OUTLAWS OF THE BRASADA

OTHER FIVE STAR WESTERN TITLES BY LES SAVAGE, JR.:

Fire Dance at Spider Rock (1995); *Medicine Wheel* (1996); *Coffin Gap* (1997); *Phantoms in the Night* (1998); *The Bloody Quarter* (1999); *The Shadow in Renegade Basin* (2000); *In the Land of Little Sticks* (2000); *The Sting of Señorita Scorpion* (2000); *The Cavan Breed* (2001); *Gambler's Row* (2002); *Danger Rides the River* (2002); *The Devil's Corral* (2003); *West of Laramie* (2003); *The Beast in Cañada Diablo* (2004); *The Ghost Horse* (2004); *Trail of the Silver Saddle* (2005); *Doniphan's Thousand* (2005); *The Curse of Montezuma* (2006); *Black Rock Cañon* (2006); *Wolves of the Sundown Trail* (2007); *Arizona Showdown* (2008); *The Last Ride* (2008); *Long Gun* (2009); *Shadow Riders* (2009); *Lawless Land* (2010); *Wind River* (2011)

Outlaws of the Brasada

A Western Duo

Les Savage, Jr.

FIVE STAR

A part of Gale, Cengage Learning

GALE
CENGAGE Learning®

Detroit • New York • San Francisco • New Haven, Conn • Waterville, Maine • London

LIBRARY OF CONGRESS CATALOGING-IN-PUBLICATION DATA

Savage, Les.
  Outlaws of the Brasada : a western duo / by Les Savage, Jr. —
1st ed.
    p. cm.
  ISBN-13: 978-1-4328-2558-4 (hardcover)
  ISBN-10: 1-4328-2558-5 (hardcover)
  I. Title.
PS3569.A826O95 2012
813'.54—dc23   2011036283

First Edition. First Printing: February 2012.
Published in 2012 in conjunction with Golden West Literary Agency.

Printed in the United States of America
1 2 3 4 5 6 7 16 15 14 13 12

ADDITIONAL COPYRIGHT INFORMATION

CONTENTS

★ ★ ★ ★ ★

GUNSTORM GHOST

★ ★ ★ ★ ★

Dan Barrister stood for a moment on the porch of Murphy's saloon, drinking in the sleepy peace of Bonito's main street. Thick poles formed a long arcade of *portales* that lined the mud-walled shops across the street. An ancient Mexican dozed against one of the poles, face hidden beneath his steeple sombrero. Up by the dilapidated stables a trio of idlers cracked piñon nuts and talked in desultory Spanish. And Barrister wished that somehow he could end his trail here, could forget the hate and loneliness behind him.

The wish was a bitter one. There had been other towns in which he had longed to stop, yet he was still wandering. He knew there would be only one end to his kind of trail. The hard glint in his blue eyes and the weather creases on his strong-jawed face gave a look older than his twenty-six years. Under a dusty ten-gallon, his hair was a startling white-blond against sun-bronzed skin. It was his gun that marked him, a big cedar-handled Colt, sagging low against faded Levi's. It had the look of being much used.

Boots thudded hollowly behind him, accompanied by the creak of batwing doors, and a big red-headed man stopped at Barrister's elbow, eyeing him narrowly. Barrister turned, waiting for the other to speak, noting the two shifty-eyed men who stood farther back—a pock-marked half-breed and a bowlegged Irishman who didn't carry his liquor too well.

"You might be Dan Barrister," said the redhead finally.

11

Barrister nodded, not surprised that the man should know him. There were always men who knew him, or of him, or of his father. It had become a weary ritual.

"I'm Lon Preebe." The big man grinned. "Thought you was Fanner's son. He had the same big jaw, same tow-head. You're a dead ringer fer him. He and I worked together afore he took on that posse by Socorro and got dusted off. If you're as good with an iron as he was, I might give you some work here. I could use a Barrister right now."

Barrister didn't need another look at the dark-faced half-breed and the tipsy Irisher to know what kind of work Preebe offered. He said thinly: "No. I don't want a job. I'm through gunning."

Preebe looked at him a moment, surprised, then he threw back his head, laughing. "Hear that? Dan Barrister's through gunning. You jokin' with me, kid? Why, you'll never be through. It's in your blood same as it was in your dad's blood. You won't quit till you're out there under them Socorro *álamos* six feet under, right beside Fanner."

Barrister spoke through his teeth. "I'm through, I tell you, finished. And I don't want any of your damn' gun-slinging jobs."

Preebe's smile faded, his beefy face hardened. "I'll never believe that. I don't know what kind of game you're playin', but let me tell you this . . . either a man's with me in this town or he's ag'in' me. There ain't no in between. And I don't want a man as good as you with an iron on the other side, Dan. You better reconsider."

Barrister shook his head, lips white, and Preebe stepped back, smiling again but without mirth. "OK, Dan, OK. You've picked your poison. It'd be smart of you to shake Bonito right quick. I've come to dislike your presence here."

Dan Barrister couldn't control the wave of impotent anger that shook him. There had been so many towns like this, so many men like big Lon Preebe. With a choked curse, he lunged forward, thrusting his elbow into Preebe's ribs, levering his forearm across his thick stomach. He shoved the redhead into the other two and, giving them no chance to recover, kept shoving. Thrown off balance, they floundered backward down the steps. Barrister gave a final heave, crowding them ignominiously into the street, then he stood on the bottom step, waiting.

Cursing, they fought free of one another, hands flashing toward their irons. But the bright memory of Fanner Barrister held them poised there—Fanner Banister who had killed three and four men at a stand with his deadly gun. And this boy crouching on the steps was Fanner's son.

The half-breed was first to pull his clawed fingers away empty. Then the Irisher, then Preebe. Finally the redhead spoke, hardly able to grate the words past the thick anger in his throat. "OK. You got top hand this deal. But you've dug yourself that grave beside your dad, Dan Barrister!"

They backed across the street and disappeared into the livery stable.

"You seem to have made an enemy in Mister Preebe," came a cool, pleasant voice.

There was something fresh and clean about her blue calico dress, something honest in her big dark eyes. It had been such a long time since this kind of woman had spoken to him that, at first, Barrister forgot to remove his hat. When he remembered, he realized suddenly that she must have been standing there during the whole episode.

"Don't you know enough to duck behind something when those things happen?" he asked.

Her smile was nice. "I didn't realize what was happening until you all went for your guns, then I was right behind you. A distraction at that particular moment could have been fatal for you, couldn't it? So I didn't move."

His slight frown was puzzled. "Few people would have done such a thing for a stranger."

"You're not exactly a stranger, Mister Barrister."

His lips twisted bitterly—even this girl. . . .

"I'm Pearl Bevins," she said, when he didn't answer. "My father's the sheriff. He's told me all about you Barristers, told me how your dad became known as Fanner because of his gun style."

Dan Barrister put his hat back on. Would they never forget his father and that gun style? He had used an old single-action Remington with the trigger filed off, and the heel of his left palm had become one smooth callous from fanning—slapping the hammer with the left hand cocking and firing the gun all in one backward motion. It was said in places like Socorro that he could empty his gun before the other man could get one slug triggered out. It had been a deadly skill; it had turned the name of Barrister into a thing for men to hate and dread. Dan Barrister bore that name. And no one believed the son of Fanner Barrister could be other than a killer. Like father, like son.

He forced his voice to be hard. "I'm not exactly the kind of man you should be talking to on the street, Miss Bevins."

"Why?" she asked calmly. "Because you're a gunman? This is a wild, raw country, Mister Barrister. Most men are gunmen of a sort. My father has killed men. And somehow I can't believe all the things they tell of you, somehow I don't think you're as bad as you're made out to be. You're no more than a boy. And you don't look mean at all . . . only a little tired."

She cast him a strange, soft smile, then turned and went toward Pablo's *Tienda,* the little Mexican store with its scarlet *ristras* of chiles hung outside. As he watched her go, he thought that it would be ironical for him to fall in love with the sheriff's daughter.

She had only intensified his longing to stop here, a longing that had begun somewhere north of Horsehead Crossing on the Pecos. He had turned up the Bonito River, where it drained into the Pecos; he had ridden through Chisum's vast holdings in the Pecos Valley where the grass was knee-high and jade-green, where the white-faced cattle with their Jingle Bob brand were sleek and fat. The land grew even more lush as he rode up the river, and white-faced Herefords gave way to great shifting herds of black Angus, their curved horns blue-white and polished like ivory. And finally, he had come to Bonito, the town situated in the mouth of a great cañon, overlooking all this sweeping pasture land. High gray walls, stippled with piñon and scrub oak, towered over the sleepy New Mexican cow town. The only sound had been the river, gurgling complacently through its willows in the bottoms, its source far up the cañon where El Capitán thrust a huge purple shoulder at a flawless sky.

Battle interests had brought a few Yankees—Murphy who owned the saloon, its porch fronting on the cow path at the point where it widened to become Bonito's main street; Hobson who had built the two-story hotel and added onto the stables. The rest of the town remained Mexican, a row of mud-walled houses and stores running up the main street, some of them flanking lanes and by-paths that led to the river. There was still an old stone tower, grim and foreboding, its narrow slots waiting for Apaches who had ceased to raid many years before. The green grass, spreading all the way up from the Pecos, the fat cattle, the peaceful town—and now the girl.

Big Lon Preebe made good his threat that evening. Barrister had eaten an early dinner at the café and was walking back through the dusk. Light from the saloon cast yellow squares onto the street; sounds of a fiddle wafted through the busy batwing doors. But Barrister didn't want any of it, knowing there would inevitably be the men who had known his father. So he climbed the rickety stairs to his room on the second floor of the hotel.

As he opened the door to his darkened chambers, a nameless sensation of danger leaped through him, snapping from nerve to nerve like an electric current. Reacting instinctively, he threw himself violently aside, crashing into the dresser. At the same time, a shot bellowed, lead clacked wickedly into wood where he had stood an instant before.

Barrister rolled to the floor, clawing his gun free. He lay there, forcing himself to breathe shallowly, soundlessly. The darkness became peopled with eerie forms; his twitching trigger finger threatened to blast wildly at them.

The would-be killer must have been holding his breath, because he let it out suddenly with a hoarse sob. Barrister lay still, trying to locate the sound exactly. It seemed to come from behind the bed, but the window shade had been drawn and he could see nothing in the gloom. So he waited. . . .

Finally, either unable to stand it longer or thinking Barrister dead, the other man moved. His body was only a shadow darker than the gloom, bulking suddenly by the bed. Barrister's finger tightened eagerly. The booming shot drowned the other's sharp cry; a heavy body shook the floor with its falling. Barrister lay quietly for another moment, listening to the hubbub growing downstairs, waiting to see if the man were only playing 'possum.

As excited boots galloped up the stairs, he rose fumblingly to the lamp. The light fell on a thick-bodied Mexican, sprawled dead on the floor, dirty-nailed hand still gripping a wooden-handled .45. He was face down, dusty sombrero partly crushed under his head. Barrister was still standing by the lamp, looking at him, when the door filled with men and women. A stoop-shouldered man with a sheriff's badge on his faded serge vest elbowed his way in. He had a dish-like chin below a snooping nose and his dark eyes were wrinkled at the edges, knowing, wise.

"I'm Sheriff Bevins," he grunted. "Looks like you had a little fuss up here."

So this was her father, thought Barrister, watching the man squat calmly beside the dead Mexican, rolling him over. Oblivious to the excited gabble of the pushing crowd, he made a minute examination, going through all the pockets, even ripping off the soggy sweatband of the dirty hat. Finally he stood, snorting: "No identification. They never have any on this kinda job. Some *cholo* from Durango, no doubt. You have any enemies below the border?"

Dan Barrister shook his head. He saw no reason to tell Bevins that this was probably Preebe's man; the big redhead had left himself in the clear by hiring an outsider. Barrister had found it wise not to stir up unnecessary things with the law.

Bevins ordered two of the gawking crowd to carry the body out, then he shut the door, cutting off the loud talk. Dragging a chair from by the wall, he turned its back to Barrister, and straddled it.

"Your killer boy came in over the porch roof and through the window, even drew the shade to make it darker. You were a nice target in the door. Seems like there are *hombres* in this town who want you out of the way, eh?"

"All right, Bevins. So there are men in town who want me gone. And you want me gone, too. Don't beat around the bush," rasped Barrister.

"That's it, Barrister," grunted the sheriff. "You're Fanner's son. I knew him well, too well. And I've heard about you. So I'd suggest you leave Bonito by tomorrow afternoon."

Barrister's voice was husky and low at first, but it grew with impotent anger and with loneliness until it was loud, intense. "Am I damned eternally for what my father was? I'm sick of being the son of Fanner Barrister. I didn't want to fight, to gun, to kill. But men wouldn't let me alone because of the name I bore. Give me a chance, Bevins, won't you? I want to stop somewhere. I want to hang up my guns."

The lawman was incredulous. "Hang up your guns? Don't give me that, Barrister. I've got too much trouble to be saddled with a repentant gunman."

Barrister wanted to say something else, but all he could think of was: "Is Lon Preebe your trouble?"

Bevins eyed him sharply. "Yeah, Preebe, yeah. The man with the most cattle and land naturally has a controlling hand in this county, so Preebe's out to get that cattle and that land, fair means or foul. And so far I haven't come across anything foul enough to nab him. He's got a lot of little tricks. A couple of ranchers found themselves upstate on a murder rap last year. Preebe got their spreads cheap at auction. It looked fishy, looked like Lon framed the killings. But I couldn't prove nothin'. Mighty clever man, Preebe."

The sheriff rose, scraping the chair back against the wall. His face was set, uncompromising. "And I half think you know what it's all about, Barrister. I half think Lon Preebe brought you up here to work for him. I couldn't have a man with your gun talent stacked on his side of the table, son. So either you leave Bonito by tomorrow afternoon, or you meet me in the street with that gun of yours ready."

He waited a moment, as if expecting Barrister to answer. But the young man was silent, eyes on the floor. He knew another appeal would be useless. The lawman snorted and walked out the door.

Sun splashed heat and blinding light into the street the next morning. Barrister was headed for breakfast, feeling empty and defeated inside, when Pearl Bevins came out from the deep shade of the arcade in front of Pablo's *Tienda*. She was running, her face strangely drawn, her eyes wide. He caught her shoulders as she tried to brush past him.

"What's the matter? You look terrified."

"I went in for some breakfast eggs. . . ." She cast a look over her shoulder. "Pablo's brother . . . in there. . . ."

Then she had torn free of his grasp and was running through the dust to her father's office up by the stables. Barrister took a half step after her, then he turned back and ducked into the old Mexican's store. There were the usual stacks of brown sugar cones on the battered pine table, the barrel of blue cornmeal; he stumbled over a pile of *yeso* bricks that they used to whitewash mud walls. But there was no one about.

"Pablo?" Barrister called. He started toward the rear doorway, brushing aside the faded black and white Navajo blanket that hung there, answering a queer moaning sound. There were two men in the back room; one lay on a crude bunk, breathing shallowly, his white cotton shirt brown with dried blood. He was fat and dark, built like Pablo who crouched beside him, mumbling weakly. Tears streaked the old man's coffee-colored face.

"*¿Qué es?*" asked Barrister tightly. "What's the matter?"

"*Señor* Barrister, you should not come!" cried Pablo. "He will kill us all."

"Who? Who'll kill us all?" snapped Barrister.

"*Señor* Lon Preebe," quavered Pablo. "*¡El gringo rojo! Muerte mío . . . todo el mundo, muerte. . . .*"

Barrister grabbed the man, slapping him in the face to stop the hysterical flow of unintelligible Spanish. "Cut it out, you fool. What's all this about?"

He finally made sense from the mess. The man in the bunk was José Oñate, Pablo's brother, and a nester on the *rancho* of *Don* Alonzo Garcia. Last night Preebe's gunnies had shot José, leaving him for dead, but he had only been badly wounded, and

19

had sought refuge in his brother's store. Kneeling beside the man, Barrister saw that he was unconscious, but the wound was not too bad, certainly not fatal.

Barrister remembered what Bevins had said about the two ranchers finding themselves upstate charged for murder a year ago, their land going to Preebe at auction. This looked like the same kind of frame. Everyone knew how the big ranchers hated nesters; José found dead on Garcia's spread would put the finger on Garcia. And Barrister remembered the *don*'s spread, the lush grass, the black Angus cattle—it would be a nice big step upward in Preebe's climb to power. Only it had slipped. José was alive to identify the bad hats who had tried to murder him, the pocked half-breed and the Irisher, known to ride for Preebe.

It was what Bevins had been waiting for; it would finish the redhead. Yes, Bevins. . . .

The lawman's voice was dry. "Right convenient findin' you at the scene of the crime, Barrister."

Barrister turned as he rose, to look down the steady bore of a .45. "You don't think I shot this man, Bevins. It's Preebe's work. It's your chance to nab him."

"That's the way I figger," said Bevins. "But if it's Preebe's work, it's your work. Your dad once worked for Lon Preebe. Until I find different, I'll believe you do, too."

The girl stood behind her father and there was a look in her wide dark eyes that stabbed Barrister. He had at least thought that she—but what was the use?

"Don't you understand, Bevins? Pablo here wouldn't even come to you when they tried to kill his brother, that's how much he fears Preebe. He thinks Preebe'll kill us all now. Would I have been here with the man I shot, just waiting for you to come?"

"Your father'd try an' shoot his way out, Barrister. You just talk. Maybe you ain't as dangerous as they say." Bevins slipped the boy's .44 from its worn leather, sticking it into his own gun belt. Then he turned to Pearl. "You go git the doc fer José. Barrister and I have business."

Her voice was thin. "You aren't going after Preebe . . . alone?"

"Who else'd help me. Barrister's right about Pablo bein' so scairt of the redhead. The rest of the town is the same way. You know that. Now you march, Barrister. Preebe's over at the stables, saw him ride in a few minutes ago."

Yes, thought Barrister bitterly, Preebe's in the stables—waiting to hear that his murder frame had worked. And Bevins had been fighting him so long, alone, that he was blinded by his own wariness. Barrister didn't look at the girl as he passed her. His feeling for her had been hopeless from the first and he should have known it. But somehow the whole thing was filling him with a growing anger.

The town seemed to sense an impending clash—the street was empty, no dozing Mexicans under the arcade, no idlers by the stables. Barrister and Bevins walked steadily toward those stables, their dully mudding boots the only sound.

There were five men in the semi-gloom of the adobe-and-frame building. Preebe towered over the others. He turned and his look of surprise was genuine when Barrister entered at the point of Bevins's big double-action Colt. The lawman's voice was flat.

"You're under arrest, Preebe, fer the attempted murder of José Oñate."

Obviously the redhead hadn't known his frame-up had failed; he turned dead white, the words came out feebly. "Attempted murder of . . . ?"

But he regained his composure with an effort, and a sudden look of craft flickered through his close-set eyes. He whirled on Barrister.

"You amateur! So you couldn't do the job right? You had to bungle it."

And Bevins did exactly what Preebe wanted him to do. He turned automatically to Barrister. "So you were in cahoots. . . ."

That's all he got out. Preebe's hand was a white blur of movement, and with Bevins still caught off guard, the stables were suddenly filled with the thunder of gunfire. The sheriff went down, fighting his gun free and firing blindly. A .45 slug slammed Barrister halfway around and down; his shoulder felt knocked off. The other men had irons now. One of them folded up with a sick moan before Bevins's flaming weapon. The rest scattered toward the rear of the stables, disappearing into the darkness. Bevins shot after them until his double-action clicked on empty chambers. He lay propped on his elbows, gasping.

"They didn't get by me, anyway, damn 'em! And you! I might've known you was Preebe's man."

Flaring anger wiped the pain from Barrister's shoulder. "Are you that thick, Bevins? Don't you see, Preebe only said that to get you off guard."

"Shut up," groaned the lawman. "I'm too fulla lead to argue. Must've emptied his whole cylinder inta me."

Barrister's cedar-handled .44 had slipped from Bevins's belt. It lay in the hay, very close to Barrister's hand. He had it and was crawling into the building before the other man was aware of movement.

"Come back here, Barrister. I'll let daylight through you!"

"Go ahead, shoot." Barrister laughed harshly. "What good'll it do you?"

He heard the sound of Bevins, jacking out empties, the dull click of good lead shoved home. And he stiffened for the shock of the first smashing slug. But Bevins only shouted, hoarsely: "I can't shoot you from behind, damn it! Go ahead and join Preebe. And tell him I'll blast you all at once."

Bevins, lying there wounded, knowing he had no earthly chance against them all, but shouting defiance in their teeth—Barrister hated to have that kind of man think he was a rat. Lips thin with desperation, he worked past the stalls of neighing, stamping, frightened horses. There was a big red wagon at the end of the line, and he threw himself under it, listening. At first he could hear only the nervous horses. Then, a scraping, sliding sound that stopped before he could place it. But it was a man; he knew that. So he worked cautiously from beneath the wagon, searching the shadows to the rear of the stables for the source of that sound. And suddenly there was that nameless sensation of danger, leaping through him, causing a violent, automatic reaction. He rolled over on his back, and he kept rolling, over and over.

Every time he was belly up, he slammed out a shot at the gunman in the rafters above. The other returned his fire, slugs squirting sawdust in Barrister's trail. Barrister careened onto his back for the fifth time and squeezed out lead. The man above screamed, falling swiftly, thudding dully when he hit. Barrister lay quite still in the haze of dust he had raised.

There were three men left—the half-breed, the Irisher, and Preebe. Would they be together? Of course, they were always together.

Barrister crawled beneath another wagon. And what chance would he have, meeting them all at once? No chance. It would be suicide.

The back end of the stables was empty; he made sure of that. Then he slipped noiselessly to the left side, skirting the stalls again, a flitting shadow in the gloom.

OK, suicide—he didn't care much now. He had hoped it would be different here, somehow, what with Pearl Bevins. . . . But, no, he was the son of Fanner Barrister. Yes, Fanner Barrister, the man who had gunned three and four men at one stand with his deadly palm.

Barrister worked in behind another pile of baled hay. He had always wondered about fanning. Though his father had been successful enough with the style, Barrister had never favored it. Some claimed it was no good because it spoiled the aim, jerking the gun up with each slap of the palm on the hammer. Others held it was all right in close, fast work where a man didn't depend too much on aim.

He stopped, craning for sound. Well, this would be close, fast work. Three at once. He could never make it triggering. The new double-action .45s were no good for fanning. But his gun . . . ? He glanced momentarily at it, a big single-action Frontier Colt. Why not try? He loaded his gun.

The sounds he made were overheard, because Preebe's voice sounded startlingly near. "That you, Bevins?"

Barrister stopped dead. "No, Preebe, it's Barrister."

The redhead laughed harshly. "My *cholo* boy slipped up last night, didn't he? And now you're here, right where I knew you'd be if I didn't git rid of you. Damn it, Barrister, why don't you reconsider? You could be my right-hand man here in Bonito."

Barrister didn't bother to answer; he was trying to locate Preebe's exact position. At his silence, the man spoke again, anger thickening his voice.

"OK, Barrister. We're all together and we've got our guns out this time. Come and get us, tow-head. All together. Your dad might've been able to do it. Not you!"

Pain threatened oblivion. Barrister bit his lips to bring back clarity. Carefully he squeezed the trigger halfway, holding it in the firing position to free the hammer.

He lurched around the square of baled hay, half turning to face them. Their guns flamed red and blue, blinding, deafening. Lead hit him hard in the thigh, knocking him down to a twisted sitting position; their other slugs whined over his head. As he went down, his left hand was working, cocking and firing the .44 with one backward slap, cocking and firing, cocking and firing. . . . Fanning.

The Colt emptied out lead faster than ever before. The half-breed crumpled with a broken Spanish curse. The Irisher threw his gun high and screamed down into a heap. Preebe jerked to one side, still shooting.

Barrister only shifted his roaring .44 slightly, batting the single-action hammer viciously, knocking out two more slugs before empty chambers made their familiar chonk.

Gunsmoke hung thick and gray in the stables, hiding Preebe for an instant. Then it thinned, and the redhead was lowering his bloody face into the sawdust, coughing, dying. Barrister looked at the three crumpled bodies dully. He felt giddy and silly and he couldn't seem to focus his eyes. Sheriff Bevins's voice wavered out of somewhere.

"Soon's I heard the gun work I knew you was square, Barrister. I tried to crawl back right fast, but I see the deal is finished."

Barrister made him out finally, crouched against a wagon wheel, bent double with pain. "Hello, snoop nose." Barrister laughed crazily. "I'm gonna pass out in a minute . . . not dying, understand, just passing out. But before I do, I'd like to know if there are any more *hombres* in this town who object to me hanging up my guns?"

Bevins glanced at the sprawled gunnies. "No, I reckon you took care of them, Barrister."

Barrister lay back. He had wiped away the curse of his father's name by the very thing that had made that name famous— fanning. There were men crowding through the door, gawking at Preebe, talking excitedly. A woman was with them. Soft hands were supporting Barrister; there was a fresh clean smell to the blue calico he laid his head against. And Pearl Bevins's murmuring: "You can stop wandering now, Danny. Preebe owned a lot of cattle, a lot of land. It will be left free with him gone. Chisum and Maxwell made their start with less."

Bevins cackled feebly. "Yeah, an' when you git patched up, I'll help you build a great big hitch rack out in front of your barn. You can hang your guns up on that an' never take 'em down again."

★ ★ ★ ★ ★

Outlaws of the Brasada

★ ★ ★ ★ ★

I

When Emery Bandine heard the crash in the thickets, he thought it was the bull he had been following. He turned his running horse toward the sound, shaking out his rope. He saw blurred movement coming through the mesquite toward him and bent forward for his throw. Then he pulled his bronco up with a disgusted curse.

It was Chico Morales, running out of the brush on a scarred-up roan. He pulled the horse to a halt, dripping yellow lather and shaking from a hard run in the June heat.

"Revere told me you was out here somewhere, Emery," Chico panted. "You might as well quit your roundup. You're going to hand all your beef over to the Yankees. Major Nadell is in town with a troop of Union cavalry."

The sweat dripped off Bandine's jaw and drenched his linsey-woolsey shirt. "Not Major Simon Nadell?"

"That's right," Chico said. "Spanish Crossing is under martial law. Every man that was in the Confederate Army has to apply for parole, and his property is to be confiscated."

Like a man getting ready to ride a snaky bronco, Bandine settled himself more deeply into the rawhide-rigged saddle. He was six feet four without his boots on, and their heels added three more inches. His shoulders were uncommonly broad even for such a tall man. He had the lean and catty flanks of one who had spent the better part of his life on a horse, and his long legs were encased in brush-country leggings of rawhide, shiny with the grease of a thousand meals. The grueling labors of roundup had melted the flesh from him, leaving shadow-stained hollows beneath his prominent cheek bones and in the sockets of his tawny eyes. His voice, when he finally spoke, held a dogged stubbornness.

"I've been six months on this gather. I coddled those cattle like babies. I dragged some of 'em in by their noses clear from the Río Grande. I've lost five years' sleep keeping 'em from stampede. They're for my kids, Chico, and no damn' Yankee is going to take 'em from me now."

Chico's sweaty rigging creaked soddenly as he drew his horse closer, pleading: "Emery, you cannot fight this. If you don't apply for parole, you're the same as an escaped criminal. Major Nadell needs meat for his commissary and you are the only one in the country with a big enough gather. Fight him and you'll put your head in a noose."

Bandine shoved his hat back to run a hand savagely through shaggy red hair. "And if I don't fight, my kids will starve. They won't have any more chance than Catherine did."

"Emery, I know how you feel about your wife. . . ."

"If you really did, you wouldn't talk like this. If I'd had a hundred dollars, I could've saved Catherine's life, Chico. It ain't going to happen again. These cattle are all that stands between my kids and what happened to Catherine. I won't ask you to go on the drive with me. But your dad's house is deep enough in the brush so Nadell will never touch my kids there. Will you keep 'em, while I'm gone?"

Chico pulled his reins in to quiet his fiddling roan. He was typical of the brush-country Mexican, a small and narrow man, burned and dehydrated by the merciless sun of this land till he was as dark and lean as a strip of old rawhide. He wore a brush-scarred jacket and the inevitable rawhide leggings that his people called *chivarras*, pouched at the knees and so worn across the seat they looked chalky. In the shadow of his immense straw sombrero, his eyes held a luminous gleam as they studied Bandine. Finally he reined his horse over and put his sinewy hand on Bandine's shoulder.

"My *amigo*, it is very hard for me to remember when you and I were not riding together. From you I learned the English. I say ain't because you say ain't. I hate Yankees because you hate them. When you went to war, it was my greatest sorrow that they would not take me, too. It has been my honor to be called uncle by your children. I could not again face them if I let you go away without me."

"Flowery as only a Mexican could make it," Bandine said. The affectionate grin touched his gaunt face and then fled. "New Orleans is the nearest market for beef, you know."

"Then let us go to New Orleans."

Bandine gripped his arm in silent thanks. Then he picked up his reins and led into the brush toward his shoe-string ranch on the Frío River. They rode into chaparral that piled itself against the horizon in bank after bank, black and sullen as tiered thunderclouds. Mesquite was a matted beard on the land, the tops of its tangled foliage billowing away in a restless sea of spine and leaf. The sun sucked the fruity reek of decay from the deep layer of leaf mold covering the earth and the scent of white brush lay thick as syrup in the draws.

It was a jungle of brush that stretched for hundreds of miles in every direction along the southern border of Texas, so impenetrable in many places that it remained unknown to white men. A dry, thorny, inimical jungle that withheld itself from all but those who had spent their lives in it, with it clawing at a man and stabbing him and fighting him every foot of the way. It fought Bandine as he penetrated the thickets, only deepening the somber mood that had settled into him. It always came like this when something reminded him of his wife, for her death was only six months behind him.

They were too young to marry. He was remembering that. It had been 1861, with Bandine only seventeen, and Catherine fifteen. And everybody said they were too young. Her family had opposed it bitterly. The parson at Spanish Crossing had refused to perform the ceremony. But they discounted the painfully early maturity that came to a boy raised in such a wild land, and in such deep poverty as Bandine had known. He was already over six feet tall, with a man's weight and a man's drive. When he and Catherine eloped to San Antonio, the justice of the peace there thought he was twenty-six.

There was a growing market for beef at the time, with outlets at Matagorda Bay and Galveston. Bandine preëmpted three hundred and twenty acres on the Frío, and Chico and his father helped build the adobe house and rode with Bandine on the roundups in the free range to the west. Bandine had already driven one herd to market when Fort Sumter fell, in April of that year. They were too deep in the brush to feel the effects of the war at once.

Their first child was born in November, a boy, Rusty. Their second was on the way when the Confederate conscript law took Bandine into the Army in May of 1862. He served with the Texas Brigade until Brown's Ferry, where a Union soldier Bandine never saw put a Minié ball through his leg. After that there were lost months in a Southern hospital, trying to save the leg. When he finally returned home, he was still weak and suffering with his wound, unable to ride or to work his cattle. Unable to do anything but sit in the sweltering heat of the dooryard and watch Catherine out in the fields, plowing and weeding and picking and shucking and bringing in the meager harvests that kept them from starving to death.

In June they learned that the third child was on the way. By November Doc Simms was telling Bandine that Catherine would have trouble with this one. The hardships of the recent years had taken too deep a toll. There was anemia, and malnutrition, and other complications that made a hospital mandatory. During those next three months Bandine would have sold his soul for enough to send Catherine to San Antonio. But he could get it nowhere. Catherine's family had no money; the brush people had been hit hard by the war, had been living off the land for the past two years. A hundred of them couldn't have raised $5 in hard cash.

On January 10, 1865, Catherine died, giving birth to a baby that never took a breath. . . .

"My friend," Chico said. "We are here."

Bandine looked up in surprise, realizing how long he had been sunk in the black despair of his memories. They had reached the river, lying sullen and brassy under a fading twilight. They turned to follow it north a half mile through dense bottom-land brush until they came to the thickets that bordered Bandine's small outfit. It was already growing dark, and the adobe house looke█████ a patch of buckskin hung against the somber backdrop of brush. Light from its two bottle windows spilled a diffused glow against the dusk, running along the corral poles in three silvery tracks that faded and died in the satiny darkness.

"Think I'd better take a scout around?" Bandine asked softly.

"Perhaps," Chico murmured. "All of Nadell's troops are Northerners and know nothing of the brush. He asked Dan Holichek to help."

"Holichek," Bandine said bitterly. "That damn' copperhead. If he's with the soldiers, he won't be coming here. He knows where my corrals are."

"Then we had better hurry," Chico said.

Bandine told him to stay and keep watch, then scouted a circle around the house. Everything seemed undisturbed. His wagon team was cropping peaceably at the fodder in the pen; the milk cow's bell tinkled softly from the brush. He dismounted at the wall of the house and looked through the line of empty bottles that formed the window glass. It gave him a warped picture of the interior, bringing back the dark thoughts of Catherine again, with its intense poverty. The floor was hard-packed dirt, the beds merely straw-ticked bunks built into the wall, the few blankets tattered and worn and held together with buckskin and linsey-woolsey patches.

The children were playing with a broken doll on the floor and Adah was sewing by the light of a sputtering bayberry candle. She was a gaunt, work-worn woman with stringy hair and knobby hands—Catherine's spinster sister who had come from her parents' home in Austin to tend the kids after Catherine's death. Bandine had to stoop through the low door, and Kit jumped to her feet as she saw him, running to him with a wild whoop.

"Daddy, Daddy, Daddy . . . !"

He caught her up and swung her ~~over his~~ head, kicking and squealing. She was the baby, two and a half years old, chubby and pink and yellow-headed. Rusty was a year older, with a pug nose and a mop of hair the same color as Bandine's. As usual, he hung back, his eyes wide and solemn in a face spattered with freckles. But Bandine strode to him and picked him up and set them each on an arm, with Kit pulling at his hair and pinching his nose and laughing uproariously.

"It's about time," Adah said. "I bet that's the first smile you had today. Anybody see you now, they'd say you was too young to be the father of such big kids."

Bandine's impulsive smile had momentarily robbed his bony face of its hollow-cheeked somberness. But now the humor faded, the stoop returned to his shoulders. He lowered the children to the floor, taking a deep breath.

"Takes time, Adah," he said tiredly. Holding each child by the hand, he walked them over to a sagging bunk, lowering his great frame into it. He cuffed off his hat, running a sinewy hand through the sweat-drenched mane of bright red hair. It struck him poignantly that this would probably be the last time in three or four months that he would see his kids. He was going to have this minute with them, and the hell with Holichek and all his bluebellies. He took Kit on his knee, winding his fingers through the yellow curls.

"Now," he said, "what happened today?"

Kit giggled. "Moo-cow in a bog, all day long."

Bandine raised questioning eyes to Adah, and she snorted: "Wasn't all day. I went out and pulled her free with a rope."

Bandine turned to Rusty. "What was it today? Yankees or Injuns?"

"Semteem Injums," Rusty announced pompously. "Kilt 'em all with my six-gum."

"Grampa Willoughby," Kit squealed, pounding on Bandine. "Grampa Willoughby. . . ."

The smile came to Bandine's face again, and he nodded sagely. "How about the time Grampa outgrinned Davy Crockett? Davy was a pretty severe colt, and quite a grinner in his day, too, you know. Once he grinned the bark right off a tree. It took him all night to do it, which made Grandpa Willoughby pretty disgusted when he heard about it, since he rarely took over an hour for such minor feats of grinning, but it still was something no ordinary grinner could do. It was that same year Grampa ran for Congress against Davy Crockett. They were supposed to speak at Whortleberry Junction, but when Grampa arrived, Davy was already up on the stump, claiming he could cuss dirtier, jump sideways farther, leap in the air and knock his heels together more times before he hit the ground, kill ornerier varmints, and hornswaggle more Yankees than any other candidate running. It was right then that Grandpa Willoughby ups and says . . . 'That well may be, but just how do you fare when it comes to grinning?' "

"Emery," Adah said sharply.

Bandine looked up at her. Then he heard it, too. His horse had begun snorting and fiddling outside. As he started to rise, still holding Kit, the door was flung open and Dan Holichek was silhouetted there.

"Hold still, Bandine. I've got a gun on you and ten soldiers outside."

II

Spanish Crossing was an adobe town. Its streets were adobe, viscid as glue in the wet season, hard as cement in the summer. Its fences were adobe, walls two feet thick built as protection against Comanche attacks in the earlier days. And its buildings were adobe, four blocks of them standing shoulder to shoulder along Cabildo Street, the main thoroughfare of the town. Many of them were part of the fort that had been built a hundred years ago to protect the Spanish colonists and the gold trains that forded the Frío here on their way between Mexico City and San Antonio. The military chapel in which the soldiers had worshiped still stood at the corner of Fourth and Cabildo, and the old *calabozo* was still used as a jail, frowning down from the high land west of Martinez Alley.

Claire Nadell could see both these ancient structures from the window of her sitting room in the inn, on the corner of Second and Cabildo. She stood in her dressing gown, doing up the enamel-black plaits of her hair, while her father trimmed his mustache before the Adamesque mirror on the bureau.

"Do you think Holichek will get Bandine?" she asked.

The clip of scissors went on with military precision. "Holichek knows the brush. He's the only one in town I can trust.

You've seen how bitterly the rest seem to hate us. I'd hoped it would be different."

She pursed her lips thoughtfully, hands stilled for a moment. It was a bitter homecoming, she thought, to find so many friends turned against you. Claire had been born on the Nadell plantation, fifteen miles south of Spanish Crossing. Her father, a West Point graduate, had sustained a wound in the Mexican War that forced him to retire. He had turned to the law and had finally brought his family to Texas in the early 1850s. He had opposed Secession from the beginning. After Sumter, when it grew dangerous for Unionists, he had been forced to flee north with his family. He had offered his services to the Union and had been given his old rank back. Upon learning that General Granger was to have the military occupation of Texas, Nadell had obtained a transfer to Granger's command and, as soon as the general had learned of his origins, had been assigned to command the Spanish Crossing district. And Claire had returned with him.

She was a tall girl, for seventeen, with a woman's maturity already beginning to fill out her body. There were deep and vivid currents in her that came to life in her gray eyes. Her lips were ripe and full, and the shape of them when she was thoughtful gave her a faintly petulant look. She was thinking of Bandine now.

"If there are so many cattle running the brush, why pick on him?"

Her father answered mildly: "Because my troops aren't cattlemen, and what men are left in town won't turn a hand to help me. Don't feel sorry for Bandine. He's merely taking advantage of a situation. For three years, my dear, almost every able-bodied man in Texas has been away fighting the war. Those cattle increased like rabbits, with not a soul to herd or brand them. I must have heard a dozen different versions of why Texans call unbranded cattle mavericks, and I guess there must be a million mavericks, anywhere from one to five years old, between here and the Río Grande. It would be utterly impossible to find out who owns them. You know it's always been the custom that any unbranded cattle over a year old belong to the man who catches them. The whole thing is a mavericker's paradise. Bandine just got the jump on everybody else, that's all."

She half turned, to look at him, knowing this was a distasteful task to him, despite his rationalization. He was a tall and lean man, a little stooped, with the high brow of the intellectual and eyes that always seemed to gaze serenely into great distances, as if caught up in some dream. One of his dreams was to dispel the bitterness and hatreds of war and bring peace back to his beloved country as soon as possible; it was why he had worked so hard to be sent back in his present capacity. But as usual, Claire thought, she had been more prepared than he for the bitterness and hatred they would meet. She had seen each meeting on the street cut into him, cloud his eyes a little more with a baffled hurt. He wanted to see only the goodness in men, and to the end of his life would be wounded and defeated by their badness.

"You shouldn't trust Holichek too far," she said. "I don't think he could have stayed here all that time without playing both ends against the middle."

"Why must you be so suspicious?" he asked. "The man is honest. He's got the clearest eyes of anyone I've ever seen."

There was a discreet knock on the door. Nadell opened it and Claire heard the crisp voice of a lance corporal inform him that Holichek and Sergeant Ayers had been sighted by the sentry. They were bringing in Bandine.

"Have them brought into the inn," the major said. "I'll have to ask you to stay up here during the proceedings, my dear."

As he closed the door behind him, she strained to see out the window. The first riders rounded the elbow turn in the San Antonio road. Dan Holichek was in front, a man who had been a part of Spanish Crossing as far back as she could remember. His origins lay in the brush, but he did not like to be reminded of it. He was always mixed up in half a dozen obscure deals— cattle speculation, freight contracting, small-time politics. She did not know how he had managed to stay out of the Army, but had heard the Secessionists in town accuse him of Union sympathies and call him copperhead behind his back. He was dressed in civilian clothes, striped trousers stuffed into jackboots, a linsey-woolsey shirt stretched across the broad planes of his chest. His face was boldly framed, something primitive to the blunt prominence of broad brow and cheek bones. Vivid little lights danced through his eyes and they were as jet black as his matted spade beard. Behind him came the linchpin wagon with Emery Bandine driving.

There was no mistaking his towering figure. The strong sunlight glinted on the edges of his hair, beneath the hat brim, and turned it to curly red flames. Beside him sat a woman Claire recognized as Adah Breckenridge, Catherine's sister. Before the war the Nadells had been distantly acquainted with the Breckenridges, and Catherine had visited the Nadell house several times. Even with this casual acquaintance, Claire had immediately sensed when Catherine fell in love with Bandine. She seemed to have matured overnight, to have blossomed, and there was a glowing radiance to her. And though Claire had been but a child at the time, she had understood, with a child's intuition, how deep and adult was the love between Catherine and Bandine.

Thus she realized what a terrible blow Catherine's death must have been to Bandine. As he drew nearer, she sought its mark in his face. There was an older look to him. The distinct shadows beneath his high cheek bones gave him a brooding somberness; the humor that had always lurked in the crevices at the tips of his eyes and lips seemed to have faded entirely. It filled Claire with a sense of deep sadness, in that moment before her attention was caught up by the children.

Bandine's baby girl was a sleeping bundle in his lap, wrapped to her chin in his buckskin jacket, so that only her yellow curls were visible, tumbling all over his greasy buckskin leggings. The boy nodded on the seat between Bandine and Adah. His freckle-spattered face was buried against his father's side, and his great mop of rust-red hair made his head look comically large for his spindly body. The thought of those two motherless children forced to ride all night in the jolting wagon immediately roused all the budding maternal instincts in Claire, and she knew she could not obey her father's request to stay upstairs.

She went to the clothes closet, throwing off her robe, and got her chambray dress with the bell sleeves and full skirt, twisting and turning to hook the bodice up behind. As she put her shoes on, she heard the clank of spurs and the muttering voices through the open window, and knew the group was passing inside. She rose, tugging her dress straight, and went out. From below, her father's voice echoed hollowly into the hall, asking Holichek how he had done it. Holichek's answer held a smug malice.

"I knew the minute Bandine got wind we was after him he'd want to hide his kids with some brush family first. He expected me to head for his corrals, but I went straight to his house. Caught his Mexican friend out in the thickets, got Bandine without a bobble."

"You didn't have to bring the children," Nadell said.

"I wanted to put a couple of men on guard there, but Bandine said he wouldn't leave his kids in the hands of no damn' Yankees."

By that time Claire had passed from the hall onto the balcony that looked down into the great chamber that occupied the front half of the lower floor. She remembered its smells so well—the dank reek of ancient adobe, the pungent scent of chile peppers hung from the rafters in glistening red chains, the powdery taint of last night's ashes graying in the huge stone fireplace.

From courtroom habit, Major Nadell had taken a seat behind one of the tables, with the group standing before him. Sergeant Ayers and a lance corporal stood near the front door, their blue uniforms filmed with dust. Bandine was at the table, holding both kids in his arms. Adah fumed on one side of him, glaring like a ruffled hen at Major Nadell, while on the other side slouched Chico Morales, his dark face haggard from the all-night ride.

There was something a little gloating about the way Holichek was paring a cigar with his penknife. He sent Bandine a sly glance, and then turned and walked to a chair at a nearby table. He sprawled into it, thrusting his dirty jackboots out before him, and lit his cigar. Major Nadell ran a finger across his mustache, nodded at Sergeant Ayers. The sergeant stepped forward, clearing his throat.

"The charges are failure to report for parole, and secreting property subject to surrender under orders issued by General Gordon Granger at Galveston, July. . . ."

"All right, Sergeant." Nadell waved his hand, settling his clear gray eyes on Bandine. "How do you plead?"

"Not guilty. How about some breakfast for my kids?"

Nadell's lips grew stiff. "Bandine, you are up before a military court."

"He's right, Father," Claire said sharply. "You haven't got any right to make the children suffer."

They all turned quickly to look at her, where she had stopped halfway down the stairs. Holichek lowered his cigar and into his black eyes came a dancing and purely male appreciation of her. All the dogged defiance fled Bandine's face; he stared up at her with a gaping jaw. She knew why he was so surprised. When she had left, she had been only a gangling pig-tailed girl of thirteen. She suddenly realized how high the square bodice lifted her breasts, how tightly it sheathed her waist. It angered her that their stares should make her conscious of such things, and she felt color rise to her cheeks.

"I thought I told you to stay upstairs?" Nadell said.

"Somebody had to take care of these kids," she told him. She walked on down the stairs and moved past the confused sergeant, arms held up for Kit. "Why don't you let me take them to the kitchen while you settle this? There's a bed in there and Poppa Lockwood can fix them some breakfast."

Adah moved protectively in between Bandine and Claire, her face set in an old maid's peevish anger. "We can take care of our own, thank you."

"Then why did you let these fools drag them all over Texas in a rattly old wagon when they should have been home in bed?" Claire asked angrily.

"I didn't have nothing to do with it. . . ."

Nadell tapped the table with a spoon. "Ladies. . . ."

"And now you don't even want to give them anything to eat," Claire said.

"Not your Yankee poison," snapped Adah.

"Maybe I better settle this," Bandine said. He stepped between them, towering so high Claire had to turn her head up to look into his face. He was not smiling, but there was a suspicion of mischief in the tawny lights running through his eyes. He lowered Rusty into Adah's bony arms. "One for you," he said gravely. Then he gave Kit to Claire. "And one for you." Suddenly, for an instant, his mouth crooked up at one corner. "Now. Does that smooth the feathers?"

For a moment she found herself staring squarely into his eyes. The humor fled his face and something veiled and disturbing hung between them. "Yes, Emery," she said. Her lips grew full and heavy. "That's fine."

"Very well," Major Nadell said dryly. "May we continue with the trial now?"

Claire wheeled away from Bandine and walked to the kitchen door, asking Poppa Lockwood to heat up some milk and to make some cornmeal mush. The paunchy old innkeeper had been watching the proceedings from within the door, and he turned toward the brick fireplace for the mush. Rusty was awake now, and Adah set him on his feet, leading him reluctantly after Claire.

"Now, Bandine," Nadell said. "I'll waive your failure to report for parole if you'll try to work this out with me. You are reported to have the only gather of beef in the vicinity, and in this case I must comply with the order to confiscate. Will you please tell us where the beef is?"

Bandine was wearing immense cartwheel spurs. Their metallic clatter echoed through the high-ceilinged room with the stir of his boots. "I don't have any beef," he said.

Claire saw the little white ridge appear about her father's compressed lips. She knew how intensely he was trying to preserve his temper. "Bandine," he said carefully, "I'm trying to meet you halfway. The war's over. It won't do us any good to go on fighting each other. There will be more troops coming into San Antonio next week. I've got to set up a commissary for the whole district. My men are on short rations as it is."

"We don't eat so good ourselves," Chico said.

Nadell wheeled sharply toward him, mouth open to say something. Then he clamped his lips shut, turning slowly back to Bandine, not speaking again till he had himself under control. "I wouldn't do this if I could establish my commissary any other way. But the town has done everything in its power to block me. I must have that beef, Bandine."

Claire saw Holichek remove the cigar once more from between his lips, watching Bandine closely. But Bandine stood without speaking, his great shoulders held in that stooped weariness, the morning light coming dimly through the slot-like windows and settling vague shadows into the gaunt hollows and crevices of his face. Claire could see her father struggling with a baffled anger, and knew a great pity for him. Again he was out of his element, brought up against the raw and willful forces of a man that he couldn't capture and sort out and catalogue in a carefully phrased legal opinion. When he at last spoke his voice had a brittle sound.

"You refuse to answer?"

Bandine did not speak. Adah made a pleading little sound, beside Claire, but it died in the silence of the room. Suddenly Major Nadell's chair shrieked against the puncheon floor, as he shoved it back, coming sharply to his feet. He stood with both hands flat on the table, the spots of color dyeing his cheeks.

"Very well, Sergeant. Lock them in the jail. And if you haven't decided to talk by sundown, Bandine, I'll put you in irons and send you to Huntsville."

III

A sound like the whisper of dry leaves in a wind struck Bandine as he stepped through the doors of the inn, behind the sergeant. He halted in the deep shade of the adobe arches, surprised to see the crowd that had gathered. It was their sound, their voices, an undulant mutter that ran back and forth down the sun-drenched street and seemed to form a sullen pressure against the adobe buildings. Bandine recognized Revere, the half-breed, and several other friends in the group of Mexican brushpoppers gathered before the Martinez house, directly across the street.

Farther down, O'Hara was standing beneath the overhang of his *cantina,* thumbs tucked officiously into his flowered galluses, surrounded by half a dozen white men too old for the war. Another knot of men stirred restlessly about the blacksmith, in front of the livery.

Behind Bandine, Chico laughed softly. "Looks like all your friends are throwing a holiday, Emery. I wonder what they're up to?"

"They ain't got any right to do this, Emery!" O'Hara shouted. "You ain't subject to parole. You been out of the Army a year."

"Maybe you want us to do something, *amigo,*" Revere called.

"How about another Bull Run?" cackled one of the old men.

An apprehensive frown touched Sergeant Ayers's sun-reddened face, and he called to the men in the street: "Break it up, now! Go about your business!"

The lance corporal crowded against Bandine's back, trying to push him on out. But Bandine refused to budge, looking back over his shoulder at Adah and the kids, still standing by the kitchen door. Chico saw the angry lights kindling through Bandine's tawny eyes and grasped his arm.

"You got to take it, Emery."

"I can't just leave them, Chico."

"Adah's there. Everything is all right. There's too many soldiers to fight. You would only make it worse for the kids by trying something. . . ."

"Corporal," broke in Ayers, "form a detail and clear this street."

The corporal pushed by Bandine and began to rattle off names. Half a dozen of the troopers lounging under the arches formed into a line and moved out at his command. The crowd knotted up across the arches gave sullenly, moving out into the street. Seeing the antagonism in their faces gave Bandine a leap of hope. Could that be what was in their minds? If they felt like this, they must already hate the occupation. Maybe he wouldn't even have had to be their friend. Maybe they would do it for anybody, just out of spite. His hope grew as he saw O'Hara now moving through the crowd, stopping here and there to speak to a man. He said something to Revere and the half-breed caught another man's arm and drifted down toward Third Street. Then O'Hara stepped into the shadowed recess of the Martinez doorway, talking to Antonio, the ancient and weazened Martinez retainer. The old man nodded to the saloonkeeper and disappeared inside. O'Hara looked across at Bandine, and then headed down toward the livery stable. Chico had seen it, too. He met Bandine's eyes momentarily, and then pursed his lips and looked skyward in a roguish prayer.

The sergeant and the corporal had been too busy trying to break up the immediate crowd to notice the pattern of movement farther out, and now Ayers waved a hand at Bandine without looking at him. "Let's go."

It was apparently his intent to march down the center of Cabildo and turn east on Fourth, climbing the hill to the jail. But the men from the livery stable and O'Hara's *cantina* had pressed in closer till the crowd was banked densely against the walls and hitch racks on the west side of the street, calling raucous comments about bluebellies and carpetbaggers. Their threatening presence gradually swelled out into the street, forcing the line of marching troops farther toward the east side and the Martinez property. Flanking the tile-roofed Martinez house on the north side was a large patio, fronted by a six-foot wall that ran for three hundred feet along Cabildo. And set in the wall, almost at its end, was a small garden door.

"Look at those bluebellies sweat!" one of the old men called. "You'd think they was marching to their own funeral."

"How about Chancellorsville?" another cried. "Who's Fighting Joe Hooker?"

One of the younger soldiers could not keep himself from answering, and turned to shout: "Better than Pickett! How about Cemetery Ridge?"

"Calhoun!" bawled the sergeant. "Keep your mouth shut."

But it was all borne along on a rising tide of tension that filled Bandine with a reckless certainty of what O'Hara was planning. The troops moved in a nervous skirmish line behind Bandine, their faces stiff and set as they sought to ignore the jibes and insults of the crowd, prodding with their rifle butts at anyone who got too near. Bandine saw a man emerge from the inn behind and quarter quickly across the street. It was Holichek, chewing thoughtfully on his cigar. He raked the crowd with a speculative glance as he pulled up beside Bandine.

"I've been talking with the major. He said half the beef would do. You could keep the other half and have your parole."

Bandine spoke with eyes straight ahead. "It always makes me vomit to talk with a copperhead."

A deep flush instantly ran up to the roots of Holichek's black hair, and the rage danced like quicksilver through his eyes for an instant. Then a slow grin parted his lips, and he reached up to run his thumb roughly through his matted spade beard.

"You know nobody can make me mad, Bandine. It's like the major says. The war's over. The sooner we forget it the better. Now, if you're smart, we might work something out. I might find a market for that other half of your beef. . . ."

"I won't make a deal with you or Nadell or anybody."

The flush returned to Holichek's swarthy cheeks, and he turned a disgusted look on Bandine. They were just opposite the little door in the Martinez wall, and a shout from the north end of Cabildo made them both look that way. A wagon came into view, careening around the corner of Third and racing down the main street toward the troops. Revere and the other man were rocking back and forth on the seat, shouting wildly.

"It's a runaway!" someone in the crowd yelled.

The knots of men gathered along the west side broke before the threat of the oncoming wagon, sweeping across the street and against the troops in a loosely packed throng. For a moment the soldiers were thrown into a panic by the shouting mob and the wagon descending upon them at a breakneck pace. It was all a whirl of violent sound and movement, soldiers and townsmen mingling together in wild eddies.

Bandine shouted at Chico and lunged for the garden door. A trooper tried to tear himself free of the mob and stop them. Bandine hit him at a run and carried the man up against the wall. Chico came in from behind and tripped the soldier, and the man went down.

At the same time Holichek plunged free of the crowd, quartering in on Bandine and hauling his gun. Bandine spun around and flung himself against the man, driving a blow at Holichek's stomach. All the air left Holichek in a sick gasp, and he doubled over. Bandine tore the gun from the man and wheeled around to see that the little door was open, with Chico already going through. Bandine leaped across the downed soldier, kicking aside his pawing hand, and followed Chico into the patio. The door was slammed shut and the bolt shot home by Antonio.

"The alley," the old retainer said. "O'Hara, he tell me. Back of the stables. . . ."

As Bandine ran across the flagstoned patio there was a battering against the door and the wall, as if a segment of the crowd had been thrown against it. Then Holichek's voice rose huskily above the other turbulent sounds.

"Ayers, they got through that door, get your men free, down through the alley . . . !"

As Bandine and Chico scaled the back wall, there was a renewed battering at the door, a different sound, gun butts against solid oak. The two men dropped off the wall into the alley and saw the saloonkeeper holding a pair of nervous horses behind the stables half a block down. As they reached him, they heard running feet down the narrow passage between the Martinez house and the next building. Bandine clapped the saloonkeeper on the back.

"You're a man to ride the river with."

"Save the thanks and get out of here," O'Hara said. "I got to get back in my saloon and look innocent."

The two men swung aboard and spurred their horses across the alley and into the ruins of the old Spanish fort, dodging crumbling walls and heaps of rubble. As O'Hara ducked into the stables, the first trooper appeared in the alley from the slot between the two buildings. He shouted and tried to get his rifle up to fire, but both Chico and Bandine drove their horses into a gaping door of the old barracks, cutting themselves off from his sight before he could shoot.

They clattered down through the gloomy, deserted building, jumping fallen beams. Then they emerged onto the parade ground, ran out through the sagging gate and into the brush. They rode the thickets without seeking a trail, pushing their animals till the sweat dripped off them like rain water and foamed up around their snouts thick enough to shave with. Finally they halted, trying to hear sounds of pursuit over the roar of the animals' breathing.

"I think we're free," Bandine said at last. "Those soldiers don't know the brush. You go on and get the cattle started toward the coast, Chico. I'm going back after my kids."

Chico's mouth gaped open. "Emery, not after you just got away. They're probably mad enough to shoot you on sight."

"And the last place they'll look for me is right back in town. I ain't leaving my kids with no damn' Yankees. But I got to get my cattle moving before Holichek finds 'em, Chico, and I can't be in both places at once."

"Bandine," Chico said. "When it comes to your kids, I think you are crazy."

Bandine hid in the thickets outside town until night. Finally dusk came, thickened by the penetrating sweetness of huisache. Bandine marked the shadowy patrol of a sentry across the front of the inn, the firefly wink of cigarettes from before the buildings in which the troops were quartered.

If they had kept the kids, the logical place for them to be was at the inn. But Holichek had caught him before by using his kids as bait, and Bandine did not think Nadell would overlook the possibility that he might come back again for them. He took off his immense cartwheel spurs and hung them on his belt so they would not betray him, then worked his way down the alley behind the inn, using spindle fences and outlying corrals for cover. He saw a sentry making his rounds at the rear of the inn. He waited till the man had reached the other end of his march, then quickly scuttled through the brush to the corner of the inn wall.

Crouching there, he pulled the gun he had taken from Holichek. It was one of the Navy revolvers Colt had brought out during the war, a cap-and-ball, lighter than the earlier .44. Bandine checked the loads from force of habit. The silvery slugs were seated snugly in their chambers.

The crunch of the approaching sentry's feet flattened Bandine against the wall. The man stepped from behind the corner. He caught Bandine's motion from the corner of his eye and started to wheel and cry out. But Bandine's gun caught him across the base of the neck before any sound had left his gaping mouth, and he slumped silently to the bottom of the wall.

Then Bandine moved swiftly around the corner and into the inn yard. He caught the awful reek of perique, the Louisiana tobacco Poppa Lockwood used in his pipe, and saw the old man having his after-dinner smoke beneath the oak. Lockwood whirled as Bandine came up from behind.

"Emery," he gasped. "You're an Injun."

"Where are the kids, Poppa?"

The old man was on his feet now. "Don't be a fool. They actually didn't expect you to come back, but they ain't taking any chances. They've got guards all around, Emery. You'll never make it."

"Where are the kids?"

The man made an exasperated noise. "Up in the major's room. That daughter of his took a shine to the tykes. Got Adah and them right with her. The major's down in the dining room having his nightcap. . . ."

Bandine squeezed his arm. "Go into the hall where I can hear you from upstairs, and, if the major starts to come up, you get a real hard coughing fit."

Before the man could answer, Bandine wheeled toward a bench, carrying it over to the wall, climbing up on it to gain the top. He worked his way along the wall to the kitchen roof, bellied up across the broken tiles till he was level with the second-story balcony that ran across the rear of the building. Once on this, he moved silently down to the lighted windows. Reaching the first one, he had his view into the room. It was meagerly furnished, with a great tester bed of hand-carved oak brought north generations ago by some Spaniard, a couple of rickety cane chairs, a cracked mirror over a side table that bore a stained china crock for water. The sputtering light of hog-fat candles fell sallowly across Claire, seated like a child on the bed's huge feather tick. Kit was cuddled sleepily in her lap, and Rusty sat beside her, looking up into her face with his solemn eyes. Adah sat stiffly in one of the cane chairs by the wall, lips pursed in sour disapproval, her sewing held motionlessly in red-knuckled hands.

Claire was telling the children some kind of bedtime story, her voice coming clearly through the half-opened window. "And this bear, he was the biggest, growlingest, furriest bear in all the world, and he had all the fuzzy little rabbits afraid of him. . . ."

"Tell us Grampa Willoughby," Rusty said.

"Maybe I better do that, ma'am," Bandine said, pushing the window open and stepping over the low sill.

Claire stiffened, her face blank with shock. Adah stood up, dropping her sewing. Kit turned in Claire's lap, then almost fell on her head, scrambling off the bed and running to Bandine.

"Daddy, Daddy, Daddy. . . ."

Bandine lunged for her in a long stride, scooping her up with one hand over her mouth. He held her against his chest and took his hand off, and she buried her face into his greasy buckskins with a happy gurgle. Rusty had turned to stare at Bandine, hanging back as always, seeming to ponder this new turn of events as solemnly as a judge weighing the facts of his case. Over the tousled mop of his rust-colored hair Claire was looking at Bandine with wide eyes. There was a satiny texture to her faintly parted lips. Finally she said: "You were a fool to come back. A score of troops in the plaza, my father and his officers right downstairs."

"You wouldn't call him, ma'am."

"What if I did?"

He took the revolver from his belt. Claire stared down the muzzle of the gun with anger darkening her eyes. "You wouldn't dare," she breathed.

"I'd do almost anything for my kids, ma'am."

After that, for a moment, it was only the sound of their breathing in the room. Then Bandine hunkered down, still holding Kit against his chest, saying softly to Rusty: "How about topping that bronc'?"

The boy considered this judiciously for a moment. Then he crawled to the edge of the bed and dropped off and came to Bandine. He climbed up on his father's knee, squirmed atop a shoulder, finally got his legs astraddle Bandine's broad neck. As Bandine rose, still holding Kit to his chest, Claire glanced angrily toward the door. Bandine stiffened, thinking she meant to call out. But she settled back into the feather tick, turning toward him again. Her lips pressed together, growing full and heavy. A smoky softness came into her eyes.

"Very well, Emery," she said. "Who could turn you in, with those kids in your arms?"

He did not smile, but the deepening crevices at the tips of his lips gave him a momentary hint of wry humor. "Yes, ma'am," he said softly.

Slowly, almost indulgently, the smile came to her pouting lips. "I think you'd say that to a woman while you were sticking a knife in her back."

He lifted one long leg out over the window sill. "Yes, ma'am," he said.

IV

That year—1865—was a bitter one for Texas. The breakup was beginning, with the first thin trickle of the defeated gray soldiers starting to return. They came back to the inevitable aftermaths of war. They came back to cotton rotting in the fields, without any market, and no place to sell the hordes of unbranded cattle running the brush. They came back to renewed strife with the Unionists and the carpetbaggers and the scalawags, descending upon the South with their radical aims of reconstruction. And it was a bitter year for Claire Nadell.

She had thought she was prepared for the antagonism she would meet. But it was an insidious thing that crumbled a person's defenses. It was like a knife turned in the wound to walk down the street and see people crossing to the other side to avoid her, to see a friend's face turn wooden with hostility at her approach, to step into a store and hear the talk and movement cease suddenly, leaving a hushed wall of silence.

The Bandine incident seemed only to have intensified the hostility. During those first days after Bandine's escape the inn had teemed with people. It seemed Major Nadell had arraigned everybody in town in an effort to find out where Bandine might be and to discover those responsible for his escape. But the men on the runaway wagon claimed that a dog had bitten their horses. Antonio had only opened the garden door to see what was going on, and Bandine had plunged through and had forced him at gun point to close and lock the door. The hostler said it must have been his careless stable boy who had hitched the horses out back. It left the major baffled and helpless, knowing it had been a conspiracy, yet unable to gain any proof against those involved.

To add to Nadell's troubles, the emancipated Negroes had begun to leave the ranches and plantations, converging on the town in droves. The belief that each Negro was to be given forty acres and a mule, the even wilder story that the slaves were to get all the lands of their former masters, the childish expectancy that the Union soldiers were there to feed and clothe them— these and dozens of other rumors filled the miserable camps the Negroes set up on the outskirts of town. The streets of the town and all its approaches were lined by begging blacks, and there was a constant threat of trouble between them and the more radical Secessionists.

In the face of all this, the fate of the Bandine children should have seemed a small thing. But Claire found that she could not forget them. In the short time she'd had with them that afternoon, they had completely captured her. She knew Bandine hadn't taken them to New Orleans; he must have left them with some family in the thickets. Even during normal times the brush people lived a harsh and barren existence; the poverty they must be suffering now frightened Claire.

She pleaded with Adah to tell her where Bandine might have taken the children. But the woman was like a rock. Nadell released her from custody the day after Bandine's escape and detailed a pair of men to watch her, with the idea that she might lead them to Bandine. But one night she gave them the slip and disappeared.

Claire had only one hope left. She remembered the red sweater Adah had been knitting for Kit. There had not been enough yarn left to finish it. The woman had not been near the store after her release, but she would eventually need more yarn, and the only place she could get it was Spanish Crossing.

So Claire went to Leander. He was the son of the Nadells' former Negro cook, Pearl, and had been lucky enough to get a job as handy man around the general store on Cabildo Street. Claire asked him to keep his eyes open and report to her anybody out of the brush who bought a ball of red yarn.

The days passed slowly, unbearably hot through July, prostrating a country already on its knees. On the 10th of July the major got a letter from his son Webb, saying he was coming home from West Point for the summer. On the day Webb was to arrive, a quarrel arose in the brush between a returned Unionist and a Secessionist, and the major had to go out to arbitrate, leaving Claire to meet her brother alone.

The stage was due at 4:00, and, when it was ten minutes before the hour, Claire started to the station. As she approached Ewing Samuels's general store halfway between First and Second, a pair of sunbonneted women stepped from the shadowy doorway, market baskets on their arms. One was Ruby Samuels, who had been a close friend to Claire's mother before her death. Claire saw Ruby turn, saw Ruby's lips part, as if she meant to speak a greeting. But the other woman grasped her arm, saying something in a spiteful voice. Guilt ran like a spasm through Ruby's face; her head dipped till the polka-dotted bonnet hid her eyes, and she turned with the other woman back into the door. It sent a thin nausea through Claire, and she had to force herself to go on, head held high.

Beyond Fourth, Cabildo made an elbow turn and ran down to the stone bridge that had taken the place of the original ford across the river. At the turn stood the stage station, a long building with slotted windows, its crumbling adobe walls still bearing the pockmarks of Comanche arrows. The keeper was lounging on the bench by the door. When he saw Claire coming, he rose, chewing at the straw between his lips with a studied insolence, and disappeared inside. Flushing with impotent anger, Claire took the bench by herself, brushing futilely at the horde of flies that immediately descended upon her. She had not seen Webb since he had started West Point, a year ago, but the joy of his return seemed hopelessly marred.

The stage, as usual, was late. But finally the scarred old Concord clattered across the bridge and came up the last stretch of road with the dust boiling from beneath its wheels like yellow smoke. At the rear window, Claire saw her brother's face, with the narrow aristocracy of her mother in his aquiline nose, his arched brows, the almost feminine sculpturing of his lips. He swung open the door, gallantly helping another woman down, then swung to the ground himself. He was in civilians, a bottle-green frock coat and gray mole-skin trousers, a slim and elegant figure, with a dashing air about every movement. Laughingly he took Claire in his arms and hugged her till she gasped for breath. Then he held her at arm's length.

"My little sister has become a beautiful woman overnight."

She was still laughing with the gaiety and release of the greeting. Webb wrinkled his nose at the ripe stable-yard smell of the sweating horses and took Claire's arm to pull her away.

"I'm so glad you've come," she told him. "It's been awfully hard, especially for Dad. We need somebody to make us laugh. How long will it be, Webb?"

An odd expression clouded his hazelnut eyes, for just an instant. She felt a small apprehension run through her, with her old sensitivity to his moods. But he chuckled indulgently.

"A few weeks, I guess. They couldn't run the Academy much longer than that without me, you know."

"Webb, look at me," she said. His smile got stiff and a little muscle twitched in his face. She put her hands on his arms. "You were having trouble with your grades last semester. You haven't been dismissed?"

"Dismissed?" There was a definite effort to the jaunty tone he created. "How can you talk that way? The high man in his class, the future general from Spanish Crossing."

"You've been booted out. Don't try and hide it from me. I know you too well."

His pretense faded like a receding tide before her knowledge of him, and he caught her hands in his, suddenly pleading: "Sis, help me. I know the major will blow the roof off. . . ."

"What happened?" she said.

"Oh. . . ." He shook his head from side to side deprecatingly. "A little gambling, a little drinking. . . ."

"And a woman?"

"I guess so."

"Webb, why does it always have to be a woman? How could you let Dad down so badly? You know it was his dream, he sacrificed so much to get you there."

"I couldn't help it, Sis. I hate to tell the major. I know how much it meant to him. Help me. He'll take it better from you."

"I'll do no such thing. You made this mess yourself, you tell him."

But when she saw the joy in her father's face, greeting his son, her resolve began to break. She kept waiting for Webb to tell the major, at dinner, and over their after-dinner smoke. But the youth did not bring it up. He retired early, saying he was tired from the trip. The lieutenant and the rest of the staff had left, and the great dining room was empty save for Claire and her father. Finally Claire gathered the courage to tell the major. She saw his face go pale, saw the old baffled hurt rise into his eyes.

"Why couldn't he tell me himself?" he said. A thin anger began to replace the hurt. "What kind of a man is he, anyway?"

He turned toward the stairway, cheeks sucked in, lips pinched tight. She had seen the same look on his face when he had been forced to chastise Webb in their childhood—not allowing the punishment to be a reaction to his own outrage, doing it as a duty, meting out a whipping as methodically as he would mete out justice in the courtroom. With this time-honored expression on his face, he started toward the stairs. She caught him by the newel post.

"Please, Dad, not while you're so upset. Wait till breakfast. Cool off a little. I think he was more broken up about it than he showed. You know how much it meant to him, if he couldn't bring himself to tell you."

The major stood a moment, and she saw the anger seeping slowly out of his face. When they finally went upstairs, he walked directly to his room. But she could hear him pacing for half the night.

It was easier the next morning. Nobody could stay angry with Webb long. The major brought it up himself, and Webb was sincerely contrite, admitting he had acted like a fool, promising he would make it up. If the major was going to be stuck in town, with this military occupation, they would need Webb's help rebuilding the Oaks. Where could they start?

The major leaned back, frowning at the table. "You may as well know now, both of you, how things stand. We haven't got any ready cash. President Johnson has appointed A.J. Hamilton provisional governor of Texas. There's talk that when Hamilton arrives the occupation will no longer be necessary. In that case I'll be transferred. The Army will begin grading down drastically, too. The best I can hope for is a captaincy. That wouldn't go very far in maintaining the Oaks, would it?"

Claire frowned in a troubled way at Webb. He shrugged, poured himself another cup of coffee. "The last time you wrote, somebody was offering you a deal on Wolf Sink Thickets. Wouldn't that mean some cash?" he asked.

The major rose and walked restlessly to the fireplace, lighting his pipe. "Holichek said he'd get a crew together on shares and clean the cattle out of Wolf Sink. He offered to give me half the profits."

"Which wouldn't come in till he sells the beef," Claire said. "It sounds pretty speculative to me. I don't trust Holichek anyway. He seems like such an opportunist."

"Don't make him out such an ogre," Webb said wryly. "From what you wrote, he did all right for himself these last years. Seems to me he's the only one in Spanish Crossing who got anything out of the stupid war."

Nadell wheeled around, staring at his son. There was a distinct pallor to his face. Then his lips grew thin, and, without saying anything, he turned and walked out the front door. Claire rose angrily from her chair.

"You fool," she told Webb. "I thought you'd grown up."

V

Holichek was busy that summer, too. He always had three or four irons in the fire. One of them was Wolf Sink Thickets. Major Nadell had got this section of brush land in lieu of payment for representing Ewing Samuels in a contested will. It had been a valuable enough piece of property for its water situation alone. But in 1863 a severe drought had dried up most of the water holes for fifty miles to the west, driving the cattle in those areas eastward in search of water. Through the succeeding years this had put more cattle into Wolf Sink Thickets than any other part of the Spanish Crossing brush land. Yet Nadell was reluctant to make a deal.

On July 25th A.J. Hamilton arrived in the state. One of his first duties as governor was to hold an election for delegates to the convention that was to revise the constitution, writing in Emancipation and nullifying the Secession ordinance. Hamilton was a former Union general and, needing all the men of integrity he could gather around him, he wrote Nadell, urging the man to file as the delegate from the Spanish Crossing district. Major Nadell immediately put in for leave, and made arrangements to go to Austin. And Holichek thought he had lost Wolf Sink that year.

But he began to notice Webb Nadell in O'Hara's *cantina*. It was the inevitable gathering place for the idlers of the town, and the boy seemed to have nothing much to do. He showed an unusual talent for poker, and managed to stay ahead of the game for some time. One of the things Holichek prided himself on was his quick, casual ability to judge men, to see their strengths and weaknesses, and pit them against each other for his own profit. He soon saw that Webb was a boy without much core who had always been able to charm his way through life, who had such a natural attraction for women that even his own sister blinded herself to his weaknesses—although deep in her heart she must have sensed what he really was, and would someday have to face it squarely.

Holichek sat in on a few sessions with Webb and saw that the youth was not averse to employing a haymaker shuffle or a false cut when backed into a corner. If cards brought out that streak of corruption in Webb, other things might, too. Holichek began to think that perhaps he had not lost Wolf Sink after all. He called in a brushpopper named Charlie Garrison who had a flair for cards, and told him what he wanted. So one January night they rang in a marked deck on Webb and put the squeeze on him and not even his haymaker shuffle would turn his luck. The night ended with the boy signing an I.O.U. to Holichek for $300. Holichek knew what it would mean to the major if he found his boy had been gambling and had lost money they couldn't pay back, and he could see that it worried Webb. So he invited him to the bar for a drink and got the talk around to the Wolf Sink Thickets.

"Can't understand why your dad's so obstinate on that deal. He's no cattleman. He certainly doesn't plan to work Wolf Sink himself."

"Claire's been pounding at him." Webb was bent moodily over the bar, toying with his glass. "She thinks we should wait for a cash deal. Why are you so interested in those thickets anyway? There's thousands of cattle in the free graze around here."

Holichek told him that in a couple of months a man wouldn't be able to make any money on the free graze. With thousands of troops returning, the thickets would be so full of maverickers they'd trip over each other. The competition would be bitter and it would spread the profits out thin. Only a man on his own land, with the legal right to exclude all others, would be ahead of the game. An option on Wolf Sink would put a man in that position. Holichek leaned close, lowering his voice.

"I have it on good authority, Webb, the cattle market is going to boom next year. . . ."

"You heard from Big Bob?" the boy asked absently.

Some of the geniality left Holichek. Why did they always have to think he got all his information from his brother? Didn't they give him credit for doing anything on his own? But he could see how it would validate the information for Webb, and swallowed his pride. "Yes, as you know, Bob's down in Austin, right in with the big boys. He told me beef at five dollars a head this year would be going for thirty or forty next spring. Now what's the most you could expect by taking cash for Wolf Sink?"

Webb shook his head. "Probably not a thousand dollars hard money in the whole town."

"That's it. But with this option, you'd get half of every dollar I made when I hit New Orleans with those cattle. There must be five thousand mavericks in Wolf Sink, Webb. Forty dollars a head. Figure it up. Wouldn't your father be a fool to sacrifice that kind of money for a penny-ante cash deal now?"

Some of the moody indifference left Webb's face; he stared into the backbar mirror, and Holichek saw the possibilities of the thing passing through his mind. Holichek put his arm over the boy's shoulder, taking him huskily into his confidence.

"You have a way with people, Webb. I think that, if you really wanted to, you could convince your father that this is the right thing. Particularly if Claire happened to be in town shopping at the time, or something. You know what I mean. Women don't understand business. Let her get under your dad's skin and she's liable to lose the biggest chance he ever had. The biggest chance you ever had, Webb." He saw Webb frown and knew what he was thinking, and now he drew upon his shrewd estimate of the youth. "And when I say *you*, Webb, I'm not speaking of the family in general. The major will get every penny that's coming to him. But so will you, my boy."

Webb's eyes lost their youth suddenly; the surface of them took on a hard and brittle reflection as they swung to Holichek. There was something intensely selfish about it. "Are you talking about the I.O.U.?" he asked.

"More than that," Holichek said. "Infinitely more than that."

Webb smiled, a secret smile. "I like the word *infinitely*," he said.

Holichek clapped him on the back. "Then we understand each other. There's just one thing. If the major gets wound up in that convention, it's liable to be six months before he gets back. That would be too late. The maverickers would move in and bleed the thickets."

Webb asked why he didn't start the roundup right away. Holichek said he would need some assurance, some word, he couldn't just go in there and. . . .

"You have my assurance," Webb said. "It doesn't matter when the major gets back. I'll be able to convince him this is the only way. You can start roundup tomorrow, if you want."

Holichek laughed heartily. "I knew I'd read you right, Webb. If it's one talent I've got, it's seeing what makes a man tick. I never miss. No, sir, I never miss."

It took a couple of weeks for Holichek to get his crew together. He made Charlie Garrison the ramrod and registered a Scissors H with the county clerk. Then he sent Garrison into the thickets with the men. He gave them a week to get camp set up and the gather under way, and then rode out to check up.

It was late February, and the rains had begun. The land lay sodden under almost daily downpours, and for a few weeks would be more like the tropical jungles farther south. The camp had been pitched near Wolf Sink. Holichek found Garrison there, a tall and loose-jointed brushpopper, emanating the dank sage smell a man got when he spent weeks sweating his heart out in the brush without a bath. There was a strange, silvery tone to his eyes that made them glitter with an unnatural brightness, like coins winking in the sun. Holichek had spent a year with him in Mexico when Texas got too hot for a man unwilling to join the Army on either side.

The gather was coming along nicely, and Holichek started back, with Garrison accompanying him to the Laredo road. They were about to part when they heard the rattle of a wagon approaching, and pulled back into the thickets. In a moment a Negro boy riding a wheezing old mare came into view. Holichek recognized him as Leander, the son of the Nadells' former cook. Behind him came the buckboard, with Webb driving and Claire on the seat beside him. The hood of a sage-green cloak covered the enamel-black abundance of her hair, its edges lying in sharp contrast to the wind-whipped pink of her cheeks.

Holichek glanced at Garrison, then touched his black with a heel, urging it out into the trail. Webb pulled his team in sharply, surprise stamped against his face momentarily; that changed to a tight, warning expression, and Holichek sensed that the youth had not told Claire of their agreement concerning Wolf Sink. He knew he had to avert her curiosity from his reasons for being in the thickets. The Negro boy gave him the cue. Tipping his hat, he smiled broadly.

"Don't tell me somebody has finally bought that ball of red yarn, Miss Claire?"

A youthful triumph was in her smile. "They have. An old Mexican. Leander came right away. We managed to catch up with the man and keep him in sight till a little while ago. But we know he took this road."

"I think it's ol' man Morales," Leander said. "He try to sell Mistah Samu'ls one o' them wooden saints."

"Do you know where Morales lives?" Webb asked.

Holichek frowned. "Never been that deep in the brush. But if you really want to find it, Garrison and I would be glad to go with you. You're getting pretty deep in the thickets, Miss Claire, and it might not be too safe for a girl like you."

Her chin lifted and her eyes glowed. "This is my country and I see no reason to fear any part of it."

He scratched wryly at his spade beard. "I know what's in your mind. I don't expect to find Bandine with them kids, and I wouldn't care if he was there. All that was the Army's business and I just offered my help out of respect for your father. Why don't you let me ride with you? I'd like to see how those little buttons are getting along myself."

His eyes were twinkling and his grin was almost sheepish. She studied him closely and then said: "I think you mean it."

"Of course I do. Nobody can know those kids without falling under their spell. Maybe Bandine and I have never seen eye to eye, but I'd give a lot to have a couple of buttons like Rusty and Kit."

He saw all the reserve melt from her, and she gave him a full and open-mouthed smile. "You surprise me, Mister Holichek. This is a side of you I had never suspected."

He leaned toward her, sweeping off his flat-topped hat in mock gallantry. "In the blackest heart, Miss Claire, there is always a ray of light somewhere."

It took them the best part of the day to reach Morales's place, fighting their way through the thickest brush Claire had ever seen, fording swollen streams that in another three months would be bone dry, struggling through draws choked with devil's head that stabbed at the horses till they squealed and fought the bit. Later on it grew dark in the east and a rain swept in on a whipping wind and the men put on their slickers and Webb rolled down the canvas top. Garrison found signs where the Mexican's wagon had turned off the Laredo road onto a game trace, and they wheeled eastward into vast stretches of sodden mesquite and dripping chaparral. They never caught sight of the man they were following, but Garrison was a good tracker, and a wagon left more sign than a man on a horse.

Finally, in the last hours of the rain-whipped afternoon, the dense entanglements parted around a small clearing. The house set within this island in the sea of brush was typical of the land, a long building, low to the ground, adobe. Sunk over its rims in the viscid mud of the dooryard was an ancient linchpin wagon, a ragged little brush pony in its harness.

Holichek stepped off his horse and knocked at the door. After a long wait it swung open on its rawhide hinges, and an old Mexican stood there. His face was as shriveled and wrinkled as a bean pod dried in the sun, but his eyes darted across all of them with a bird-like sharpness. Though Claire had heard Bandine speak of Santero Morales, she had never seen the man before. Apparently Holichek hadn't, either, for he asked: *"¿Habla inglés?"*

"Yes," the old man said gravely. "I speak the English."

Holichek introduced himself and the others, and then told Morales they were hunting Bandine's children. The old man shook his head, saying that they were not here. Holichek asked him why he had bought the red yarn. The old man said he hadn't bought any red yarn. Claire climbed down from the wagon, lifting out the basket they had brought. She walked to the door and took the cover off its contents.

"We aren't going to harm the children. Look. We've only brought them food and clothing."

Morales frowned at them, but before he could speak, Adah appeared in the doorway behind him. The dim light left gaunt shadows in the hollows of her bony temples, and her work-reddened hands were clenched defiantly.

"You can't get Bandine this way," she said. "He ain't here."

"We aren't after Bandine," Claire said. "We went through the attic. Here's a suit my brother wore when he was five. And a dress of mine. It may be a little big, but you can fix it. And these coats. They need them, Adah, you know they do. It's already getting so cold."

She broke off as Rusty appeared from the gloom of the room, peering curiously around Adah's skirts. "Injums?" he asked hopefully.

None of them answered. They were all looking down at him. His eyes seemed enormous in his thin little face; his cheeks held a parchment-like pallor beneath the thickly spattered freckles. Adah had patched and sewn his clothes in a dozen places to hold them together, but they were still little better than rags. For shoes he had pieces of buckskin tied around his feet with rawhide thongs. He was noticeably shivering in the chill of the open door. At last Adah raised her gaze from him, to look at Claire. Her eyes were squinted and suspiciously wet.

"All right," she said. "Come in."

Claire stepped into the barren room, with the men crowding in behind her. Her first impression was of the hand-carved wooden figures. They seemed to be everywhere, standing in ranks upon shelves, peering from innumerable niches in the adobe, lined up on the floor against the wall. Claire's attention was arrested by one figure mounted on a snow-white horse, two miniature straw sombreros on his head. The old Mexican smiled shyly.

"That one is Santiago, the patron saint of Spain. I make for him two hat, you see. He come long way. One maybe would wear out before he get here."

Claire smiled, realizing why they called him Santero. He was a carver of saints, a carry-over from the earlier days when each Mexican village had its *santero* just as it had a blacksmith or a butcher. It sent a strange feeling through Claire to know that these were the things that had partaken in the molding of Emery

Bandine—the fey old man with the bird-like eyes and the simple faith of another age, this barren room with its countless wooden faces peering so fixedly from every corner. For Santero Morales had been a close friend of Bandine's parents. Bandine had been but twelve when they died, and Morales had taken the boy in and reared him as a brother to his own son, Chico.

"Where's Kit?" Claire asked the old man.

Adah answered. "She's in the back room, asleep."

But even as she spoke, the child appeared in the doorway, her yellow curls tumbled about her pale cheeks, her eyes heavy-lidded from slumber. "Kit not sleep," she pouted. Then the pout broke into a smile as she recognized Claire, and she waddled across the room, holding a statuette in her arms almost as big as she was. Claire recognized Our Lady of Carmel, her taffeta dress trimmed in blue ribbons, the sleeves puffed like a Velasquez lady's. Rummaging quickly through the basket, Claire brought out a hooded cloak of green satin she had worn when she was a child.

With a delighted gurgle the little girl set Our Lady of Carmel down and ran toward the cloak, pudgy hands outstretched. As Claire helped her on with it, Holichek moved closer, his slicker squeaking softly.

"I'll be dog-goned," he said. "If she don't look like a little princess."

Still on her knees, Claire looked up at Adah, saying impulsively: "Adah, why don't you bring them to the Oaks? Webb and I are moving out there in a couple of days. We have so much room. The kids will be so much better off there."

Adah's face grew stiff. "You think Emery would have that?"

"You'd think he'd want his kids to be taken care of decently, if he loves them as much as he seems to. . . ."

"He loves them more'n you or me or anybody else will probably ever know," Adah said. "But he's got pride for them, too.

All of Bandine's feelings run so deep and strong they scare me sometimes. When he's mad, it's like the sky dropping in. When he hates, it fair tears him apart. When he loves, it's the same. He loves those kids that way." She paused a moment, face darkening. Then she said: "And Catherine. . . ."

"I guess her death was a terrible blow," Claire said.

"Nobody'll ever know how terrible. Him just back from the war, with that wound. Not able to work, no jobs if he could work, his family starving. It wasn't nothing new to him. He was that poor all his life. Bitter poor. I'd seen him rage against it before. But never the way he did after Catherine died. He went out in the brush, just like a steer does when it's a-goin' to die. I thought maybe that's what would happen. Two weeks. Not a sign. Not a word. Then he come back. The look of him scared me so I almost ran. He was starin' right at me. He didn't even see me. His voice sounded like a tomb. 'This'll never happen to my kids,' he said. 'I swear before God, this'll never happen to my kids.' "

Adah stopped then, gazing blankly over Claire's head. No one spoke. The fire spat softly. It was as if Claire suddenly became aware of the barrenness of the room. The oven was merely a cone of adobe, molded into the wall, and its heat did not reach Claire at all. The floor was earth, packed hard as cement, and the beds were only straw-ticked bunks built along the wall. It seemed to open the door, for Claire, to all the bitterness and struggle and heartbreak that had made Bandine what he was. It made her realize that his intense reactions to poverty went back through the years, that Catherine's death was only the culmination of a lifetime of this.

She rose slowly, her cloak whispering in the silence. Before she could speak there was a shout from outside, the sound of stamping hoofs. As they all wheeled toward the door, it was flung open by Emery Bandine. He had to stoop to get through, and then he straightened, with a broad grin on his face. It died instantly, as he saw who was in the room.

"Daddy, Daddy, Daddy!" Kit cried, running to him with outstretched arms. He bent to scoop her up and hold her against his chest. Santero was right behind her, grabbing Emery's arm and pounding him on the chest like a kid so happy he could hardly bear it.

"My *hijo*," he said, "my son, I thought for sure you were not come back, it has been so long, where is the other little one?"

"Right here, *padrecito!*" shouted Chico, coming through the door. He grabbed the old man and danced him around, and Santero was laughing and crying at the same time. Bandine stood without saying a word, staring at Claire and Holichek, so tall his hat almost touched the ceiling, rain dripping off its brim and running down the stiff folds of his slicker to form dirty brown pools on the floor. The glaze of exhaustion filmed his eyes. His face was smudged with grime and a bristly beard curled its ruddy mat into the gaunt hollows beneath his prominent cheek bones. When he finally spoke, his voice was hoarse with weariness.

"Don't you ever give up?" he asked Holichek.

"It's nothing like that," Claire told him. "We just brought some things to your kids."

Bandine seemed to become aware of the satin cloak Kit was wearing. Scowling at it, he walked to the table with her, his immense spurs setting up their clatter. He stood her on the table and took the cloak off her and tossed it upon a chair. Then he pulled aside his slicker, unbuttoned his shirt, unbuckled the money belt beneath it, and pulled it from around his body.

"My kids don't need no charity," he said. He dropped the money belt on the table with a weighty clank. Then he turned to Holichek. "And if any damn' Yankee major wants to come and get this for his commissary, just let him try."

Holichek surprised Claire, showing no anger, tucking his chin in, and chuckling huskily. "The major's in Austin right now, Bandine, and martial law is about over in Texas. Nobody's going to take your money." He raised one black brow at the money belt. "I never saw such a fat one. They must be paying high for beef in New Orleans."

"High enough to go back next year."

"Be a little different than this time. You'll have competition."

"Not if I'm working my own land. I aim to have the best patch of brush in Frío County, and there won't be another mavericker on it."

"Not Wolf Sink Thickets?"

"What's it to you?"

Holichek scowled thoughtfully at Bandine, as if letting something pass through his mind. "Nothing," he said finally. Then he drew a quick little breath and looked at Claire. "I think we'd better go now. You won't get back to town till after midnight as it is."

"Very well," she said. She turned to Bandine. "Now that you really don't need these things, it surely wouldn't hurt your pride to keep them as sort of a gift for the kids."

"Ma'am," he said, "if I let my kids wear them Yankee clothes for one day, they could never hold their heads up in Texas again."

It was so droll she started to smile. Then it faded, and her underlip took on the heavy, almost petulant shape; her face grew soft and full as she gazed up at him. She could feel the insistent pound of pulse through her body. Without speaking again, she turned and went out. Webb helped her into the wagon and climbed up beside her, frowning at her.

"What's the matter?" he asked.

She knew what was the matter. She had kept a picture of Bandine, all these months, a towering man with the crevices of humor gone from the corners of his eyes, the hair curling like little flames against his temples. But now she had met the fey old Mexican with his wooden saints, had seen the house in all its stark and primitive impact, had heard Adah talk. And now the picture she had of Bandine went so much deeper than that first surface impression.

That her realization, now, should come so quickly and so unquestioningly might have seemed strange to one who did not know her. But she knew it was no spur-of-the-moment thing. It had been forming in her all these months, ever since that day she had seen Bandine at the inn, though she had not fully understood what was happening to her. But now she understood. Her need was as certain as the pound of pulse through her body, and her decision was as certain.

"What is it?" Webb asked again.

She would not have told anyone else. But despite his weakness, Webb had always been close to her, and she knew he would understand. She shivered faintly, drawing her cloak about her. "Is it right to be a little afraid of the man you want to marry?"

VI

Bandine was moody and silent through breakfast next morning. Wolf Sink Thickets was the most valuable strip of land west of the Frío. Something in Holichek's manner the day before had planted a seed of suspicion in Bandine's mind. He had planned on Wolf Sink too long to lose it now. It rankled him to deal with a Unionist. But maybe seeing a Yankee scramble on the short end of a deal was enough justification for doing business with him.

So Bandine rode up to the Oaks, standing on its height above the river, its bright red brick dark with age and disuse now, the great round columns of its Ionic portico showing the green-gold of decay at their massive bases. Claire was surprised to see him so soon, but ushered him cordially into the library. He remembered how, fifteen years ago, the Empire Aubussons had been the gossip of the country for months, when the Nadells had first moved in. Now the rugs were worn through in a dozen places, tawdry and faded. And the gilt was peeling off the girandole mirrors and the harrateen shone like worn serge across the seats of the delicate Sheraton chairs. It convinced him of what pinched circumstances the Nadells were in.

He made Claire an offer of 10¢ an acre for the Wolf Sink Thickets. She finally agreed that with the bottom out of everything his bid was probably the best they could hope for. He said he couldn't wait till the major returned to close the deal. He told her he'd guessed that they were ready to lose the Oaks without this money. She agreed miserably. Then, he said, it was almost certain that the major would accept the deal. So Bandine would gamble on that fact, would deposit the $2,500 in the bank to their credit and start roundup. If it was unacceptable to the major, when he returned, the cattle would still be theirs—it would be written into the contract—and all they would owe Bandine was two bits a head for gathering and branding. That was according to custom, and Claire finally agreed. They rode into town to deposit the money and have Jerry Waggoner draw up the contract.

All the way in, Bandine was aware of that strange expression in Claire's face. Her lips were slack and full-looking, the way they had been the night before, and she kept her eyes fixed so shiningly on his face that it disturbed him intensely.

He got back after midnight, and did not get to tell Adah and the others about it till breakfast. He said he wanted to start right away, and Chico said he was crazy, after being in the saddle all the way from New Orleans. But finally both of the Moraleses signed on with him, and they all rode out to get a crew. They signed on Revere, the half-breed who had gone to New Orleans with them and who had half a dozen neck oxen that they needed, and they looked up Lee and Billy Graves, just back from Terry's Rangers in the breakup. They had all worked for Bandine, and knew how he drove a man. Santero said he was too old for that, but would pitch camp and build the corrals and do the cooking. So they made camp on the extreme northern border of the thickets and were in the saddle before sunup next morning.

Bandine divided them into two groups, he and Chico and Revere heading east. The first of the vast thicket met them like a wall. They forced their way through tangled mesquite and white brush for a quarter mile till they found a game trail. Then the brush began to pop ahead.

"It's a bunch," Bandine said. "Let me get around in front of 'em, then drive 'em in to me."

He put the spurs to his horse and it plunged off the trail, seeking holes through the thickets. He had a dim sight of flashing bodies in the brush ahead, the chest of a black bull, the gaunt and churning hip bones of a brindle heifer. The brush was popping like cannon fire all about him, and he was making half the noise.

A dense escarpment of chaparral loomed before him. If he stopped to find a way around, he would lose the cattle. He drove his horse directly into it, knowing that, with the instincts born of a lifetime of brushpopping, the animal would find a hole. In the last instant the animal veered aside, almost unseating Bandine. But it had found a thin spot.

He charged through and out onto another pear flat, with the cattle running on his flank. He spurred his horse and quartered across the front of the charging beasts. There were half a dozen of them, brush dripping from their horns and scarred hides. They tried to veer away, crashing into a mesquite thicket. But Revere showed up on the other side, turning them back in to Bandine. It put them into a mill, bawling and making feints to escape and clattering their horns.

Bandine and Chico circled them till Revere brought up the three neck oxen to drive in with them. The tame beasts quieted the wild ones till they could be driven. Then the men pushed on. In a few minutes they heard another great popping of brush and Bandine had a blurred glimpse of a bull the color of mulberries.

"That's the biggest one I ever saw!" Chico bawled.

They left Revere to hold the others and ran the mulberry bull a mile before they caught it. They cornered it up against a wall of tangled chaparral and mesquite that looked impenetrable enough to stop a locomotive. The bull charged right into it, ripping such a big hole that both horsemen could follow through. They knew that this was a *cimarrón,* a true outlaw, and that they could never run it down and drive it like the tamer beasts. They got their ropes out and ran till they caught it in a flat, and there Bandine heeled it. The earth shook as the beef hit. Bandine's horse came to a stiff-legged halt and Bandine jumped off with his pigging strings. He threw one of these short ropes about the hind feet of the kicking, squalling bull, and cinched up tight. Then he drew its front feet in and hog-tied it. When he straightened up, he saw that there were two other men in the flat beside Chico. They had stopped at the edge of brush, Dan Holichek, on his fiddling black, Charlie Garrison on his bay.

"You're a little late, Bandine," Holichek said. "I got an option on these pastures."

"I thought it was something like that," Bandine said. "Can you show a contract?"

"Can you?"

"I've got one," Bandine said.

"How could you? The major's in Austin."

"He has the option to sign it or turn it down when he gets back. Waggoner drew it up and it's all legal, Holichek."

"You're trying to pull a double shuffle, Bandine. My agreement is a prior one. It puts what you're doing in a class with rustling. I want you out of the thickets by sundown."

"And if we ain't out?"

Garrison straightened up in his saddle. The sun made a silvery shimmer across the unnatural brightness of his eyes. Chico began to sidle his horse toward Bandine, his body tight and high-shouldered in the saddle. Then Holichek pulled up on his reins, arching in the neck of his horse painfully.

"I'll find your pens," he said. "I'll put my brand on your cattle. I'll take you into town at the end of a rope."

Chico held a tight rein on his fiddling horse, listening to the crash and pop of the brush as Holichek and Garrison rode away. Finally he turned to look at Bandine.

"The major might have really given his word to Holichek without Claire knowing," he said.

Bandine shook his head. "Hard to say. I don't think Claire would pull a fast one on us. On the other hand, I don't think Holichek would go this far without some assurance on the part of the Nadells. But I don't think Holichek has any cash. I'm sure the major will take our offer."

"Holichek ain't one to back down."

"Neither am I."

After that they went back and got one of the neck oxen from Revere, returning to the hog-tied bull. They hooked the lead rope around the bull's neck and horns, and hitched it the same way to the oxen. When they untied the bull's legs, he scrambled to his feet and started pawing and bellowing and trying to jerk free. He pulled the ox all over the clearing before he finally realized he couldn't get loose. Then the ox began to work patiently at him, moving around and around the kicking, bawling *cimarrón,* pushing him gradually toward the northern edge of the open patch. Bandine knew that it might take a few hours, it

76

might take days, but sooner or later the ox would have that bull back at the pens, waiting for its reward of burned prickly pear or cottonseed.

The men rode the day out, roping and necking the wild ones to the oxen, gathering the tamer ones. By late afternoon they had only a dozen to drive back to the pens. They killed one beef and spitted fresh ribs over the fire and mixed up some of the tallow with meal and water and salt for the cornbread. The men were dead tired from the grueling day, but Bandine could not forget Holichek, and put them all on two-hour watches, despite their grumbling.

Near midnight he was awakened by a bawling and crashing in the brush. He thought at first it was one of the neck oxen bringing in a wild one. Then he heard a shout, the crash of breaking timber. He jumped out of his blankets, grabbing his cap-and-ball from its holster by his head.

In the bright moonlight he saw that one whole section of corral fence had fallen down and the cattle were stampeding wildly through the gap into the brush. He had to veer off and stop to avoid being run down. Bill Graves came running out of the dust, cursing bitterly.

"Damn' cut of steers come out of the brush. Rammed against that fence, knocked it down. I don't see how. Got the whole herd wild."

Bandine stared helplessly at the last of the cattle disappearing into the thickets. It would take precious minutes to saddle up. By that time the beef would be hopelessly scattered for miles. At last Bandine walked down to the trampled section of fence. He found that one of the rawhide lashings had been cut. He looked accusingly at Graves.

"Did you take a nap, Bill?"

Graves tried to meet his eyes, then looked at the ground. "Emery, I don't know, I'm sorry. . . ."

The deep grooves of anger on either side of Bandine's mouth turned his face to a carved mask. "All right," he said. "Forget it. I guess somebody crawled in and cut the fence while you were asleep, and then drove that other bunch of cattle in to knock it over and stampede ours." He turned to Revere. "Can you trail that man tonight?"

"I will try," the half-breed said.

Bandine and Revere started saddling up immediately, not even waiting for the other men to dress and follow. The half-breed found the tracks and followed them on foot into the brush, where a second man on horseback had held the cut of steers they had stampeded at the pen. Revere mounted here. Bandine pushed hard, following the tracks through brush to a trail. Here they opened up into a dead run, Revere bent low in the saddle to spot where the riders had watered their horses and had taken a smoke, and knew they had gained maybe ten minutes on the men because of that. Their horses were winded and running soddenly when Bandine caught sight of the silhouettes on higher land ahead. He put the spurs to his horse.

The two men finally heard him coming, turned to look, wheeled off into the brush. It was like running cattle. The brush popped and crashed all about Bandine with the multiplied echoes of a cannonade. By the bright moonlight he caught sight of Charlie Garrison ahead, tailing the other man. Garrison veered aside fifteen yards to put his horse through a thin spot in a wall of chaparral. Bandine took a straight line, bursting through the thicker section Garrison had avoided.

It almost tore him off his horse, but he erupted on the other side to find himself right on Garrison's tail. Garrison turned again and saw how close Bandine was and started grabbing for his gun. Bandine spurred his horse broadside into Garrison's animal, and then dove at Garrison before the man had his gun free, carrying him out of the saddle.

They flipped over in mid-air and hit with Garrison on top. He had lost his gun in the fall but he came to his knees astraddle Bandine and smashed him in the face. Dazed, Bandine blindly warded off the next blow with an outflung arm and surged up beneath Garrison.

It spilled the man off, and Bandine rolled over toward him, trying to follow up with a blow. But he missed, going hard into the man, and Garrison brought a knee into his groin. It doubled Bandine over against Garrison, sickened with the pain. They were on their knees together, and Garrison hit Bandine in the face before he could recover. It knocked him over onto his back. Garrison lunged to his feet and jumped at Bandine. His face was twisted viciously as he kicked at Bandine's unprotected head.

But Bandine caught the boot in the last instant and spilled Garrison. As the man rolled over and tried to jump erect, Bandine scrambled to his feet and plunged for him. He caught Garrison half rising, hitting him in the stomach. It folded Garrison up like a wet dishrag. Bandine caught him by the shirt front before he could fall and hit him again, in the face, straightening the man up, and hit him once more, with all his weight behind it. Then he stepped back and let Garrison fall.

He swayed above the man, breathing stertorously with the pain of that knee in his groin. He looked around for the other rider but could not find him, and guessed he had run out on Garrison. As Revere burst in on them from behind, Garrison rolled over, groaning. He rose up feebly, spitting blood and a tooth onto the ground. His nose looked broken, and Bandine's knuckles had laid the flesh wide open across one cheek bone. They were marks of the fight that would last a long time, and that he could not hide.

"Take that back to Holichek," Bandine said. He had to suck in a big breath before going on. "Tell him it's what will happen every time I see one of you in these thickets. Tell Holichek the next time it'll be him."

VII

In January of 1867 Big Bob Holichek made one of his flying visits to Spanish Crossing, sending his usual telegram ahead of time to insure a welcoming committee. When Dan Holichek arrived at the stage station that morning, he found the bunch from O'Hara's already there. Ewing Samuels squinted genially at Holichek through his spectacles.

"Ain't often a man Bob's size gives us the honor, Dan. Your big brother's really made a name for himself down there in Austin."

"Yeah," Holichek said grayly. "Really made a name."

He fired up a cigar, feeling the old resentment stirring within him, the mixture of excitement and antagonism with which he always greeted one of these visits from his brother. They heard the hollow trumpeting of the stage horn before the coach came into view, clattering across the stone bridge, pitching violently on its thorough braces as the driver brought it to a flourishing halt. Samuels opened the door and Big Bob stepped down, grunting heavily as he hit the ground. He was a red-jowled, flamboyant man in a steel-pen coat of hunter's green, the diamond scarf pin on his cravat looking as big as an egg, winking and glittering in the sunlight. Dan Holichek saw the men gaping at it as they hailed Bob, clapping him on the back, pumping his hand.

"What's the word, Bob? We going to let that Secessionist governor stay in?"

Big Bob chuckled, lowering his voice confidentially. "Keep it under your hat, gentlemen. The big boys at Washington don't like Throckmorton in power down here any more than we do."

Samuels's eyes bugged out. "What are they planning?"

Big Bob spoke behind his hand, voice husky as a conspirator's. "By March, the late Confederacy will be under military occupation again. Throckmorton will be out. Pease will be in. We'll have it all our own way."

He dropped his hand and leaned back, grinning expansively at the gasp of astonishment that ran through the crowd. Then, in a swift change of mood, he invited them all to a drink at the hotel. They all trooped to the Hastings House, on the corner of First and Cabildo, with Big Bob's latest dirty joke bringing up a rough guffaw, his own booming laugh rising above the others. But underneath his expansive geniality, Dan Holichek noted the harried sense of rush that always seemed to associate itself with his brother these last years. Bob left his drink half downed and excused himself.

"You know, boys, only got a few minutes while they change the team. Haven't seen little brother in a year."

They went up to the room Dan Holichek always kept at the hotel. Bob put his gold-headed cane across the table and lifted his tails to seat himself on one of the chairs. Then he stopped, flicked a hand at the dust caking the seat, and straightened to walk irritably to the window.

"Little place," he said, staring through the flyspecked glass at the street below. "I'd forgotten how little." Then he turned to frown from beneath shaggy brows at his brother. "So you lost Wolf Sink."

Dan Holichek's expression grew sullen. Why did Bob always make him feel like a kid, caught stealing cookies? "I had it all set up. The Nadells agreed to give me an option, then backed out on their word."

"What do you mean backed out? Claire brought Bandine's contract down to Austin for the major to sign. I talked with the major. He never gave you his word on anything."

Dan Holichek flushed. "He's a liar. . . ."

"Don't try to carry it off with me, Dan. You were trying to pull a fast one and it slipped up. You talked Webb into selling out his father." Big Bob jerked a cigar from his breast pocket, gesturing angrily with it. "Oh, nobody could haul you into court over it. But it was a sell-out just the same. You knew the major's pride. He might blow his top at the boy for agreeing to such a deal. But a Nadell's word had been given, and the major would stand behind it if he lost everything. . . ."

"What are you so sanctimonious about?" Dan Holichek asked, coming to his feet and slapping the table. "I've seen you pull shadier things a dozen times a day. . . ."

"And succeed with them." Big Bob pared the end off his cigar with a penknife, snapping it angrily to the floor. "That's the point. How can I trust you to plan anything? I understand you couldn't even get the crew to stay, after Garrison came back, all beat up that way by Bandine."

"I. . . ."

"Never mind. I haven't got time." Bob fired up his cigar, puffing on it furiously, surrounding his beefy jowls with fragrant smoke. Then he began to pace. "This is something big. If you let it slip, I'm through with you." He wheeled, jabbing the cigar at his brother. "In a few months the Kansas Pacific will be through Westport, pushing toward California. It will have reached a place out in the middle of Kansas called Alibine or Abilene or something. A man named McLaine is going to put cattle pens and loading chutes there and make it a delivery point for beef. Can you see the possibilities?"

Dan snorted. "Who couldn't? It'll be the first decent chance cattlemen will have to reach a railhead that will take their cattle to the Eastern markets in big numbers. They'll be swarming across the Indian Nations."

"Not this year they won't. I've been working on McLaine a long time for this. He's made me his agent. I'm the only one south of Kansas City who knows his plans. He depends upon me to spread the word. But it won't be spread. He'll get his cattle, but they aren't going to come from every two-bit brush-popper that can drive a dozen steers across the Nations. They'll be our cattle, little brother, under our road brand."

Dan frowned, with the growing implications of it. "How can you keep something this big from leaking out?"

Big Bob shoved aside his lapel to tuck a thumb expansively in the armhole of his flowered waistcoat. "Naturally it will leak out. But if we work it right, we'll have our own cattle on the trail by the time the other cattlemen hear about it, and they'll either be on their way to Sedalia or New Orleans, or it will be too late to round up and drive before winter. McLaine says he can ship around twenty thousand this year. Can you get hold of that many?"

Dan scowled, pulling on his beard. "A lot of the soldier boys have come back and started mavericking. I guess there must be a pretty big gather in the brush all right, even though it's scattered up in little bunches."

"What can you get it for?"

"Couple of dollars a head, if it's a cash deal."

"We'll be able to get fifteen or twenty dollars a head at Chicago. Counting out wages and loss on the trail, that'll still give us a profit of ten or twelve dollars a head. That's over two hundred thousand dollars. I told you it was big. Can you get enough cash to buy here?"

Dan's head snapped up angrily. "You know I don't have that kind of money."

Bob snorted. "All right, little brother. I'll send you a check to cover it. But do it smart. Don't buy them all yourself, spread it out. . . ."

"You don't have to tell me how to make a cattle deal."

"Somebody should, you let a brush yokel like Bandine pull a

fast one on you."

"Dammit, Bob. . . ."

"Got to go now, kid. Keep me posted. Omaha till August, Chicago through September, Washington after that. Same hotels."

He scooped his cane off the table and swept out. Dan Holichek followed him down and they went with the crowd to the stage. Dan stood apart from the others, forgotten in the moment of departure. It only deepened the resentment in him. It seemed like he had been toadying to Bob all his life. Running his errands, doing his dirty work, taking lickings from him when they were kids, losing jobs to him when they were older. Losing Carrie.

His eyes went bleak and empty with the thought. He wondered if he would ever feel that way about a woman again. He had thought it was one thing he would not lose to Bob. Carrie had never actually committed herself, but there had been so much between them, and Dan had been so sure he had seen it in her the way it had been in him. And he had awakened that morning to find both of them gone, Big Bob and Carrie. He hadn't seen her since. He could never bring himself to ask, but, from the few things that had been dropped, he sensed that Bob and Carrie didn't have much of a marriage left. It didn't matter. It didn't bring her back. . . .

With the coach gone, the crowd drifted back to O'Hara's *cantina,* still talking about Bob's surprising news. Dan Holichek trailed along, gnawing at his cigar, feeling an almost uncontrollable impulse to tell them about the cattle deal. The hottest thing that had hit Texas in ten years. It would rock them on their heels. Then they'd know who the big man was, they'd know who had the real word.

He did not drink with them because he knew, if he got drunk, he would spill it. After a while they drifted off, and O'Hara's swamper was moving through the gloomy room lighting the kerosene lamps. Dan saw Webb at a rear table, idly playing solitaire. He walked back to the boy with his drink and took a chair. For a while Webb had been stiff and defensive with Dan Holichek, probably over the Wolf Sink fiasco. It had left him now, however, and he had settled back into his shallow flippancy.

"Big Bob give you a hot tip?" he asked.

Holichek's humor left him. "No," he said. "But I've been working on something, if you want in on it."

Webb's smile was lop-sided. "Always got some little deal working, haven't you?"

Holichek said sharply: "This is big. . . ."

"That's what you said about the Wolf Sink deal. But I've talked with Bandine. He said there aren't any five thousand mavericks in there. And they aren't going to bring any more in New Orleans than they did last year. I think you were just trying to use me in another one of your penny-ante operations."

Holichek felt himself flush to the roots of his hair. He leaned across and put his hand on Webb's arm, gripping it so tightly the boy winced. "Listen, you young fool. In two months, right in the middle of Kansas, there's going to be a railhead where cattle can be shipped to Chicago. Do you know what *that* means?"

He saw the boy's eyes grow momentarily wide with surprise, then cloud with suspicion. "Is that the truth?"

"Do you think I'd be sending you out to buy every head of cattle you can get your hands on if it wasn't?" Holichek asked.

Webb's mouth gaped open. "Me?"

"Yes," Holichek said. "I need some agents."

The boy was shaking his head, a wondering look in his eyes. "The brushpoppers will go crazy. Bandine will be rich. I hear he's got over a thousand in his gather already. . . ."

"Bandine isn't going to sell. Nobody is. Every head of cattle that goes north is going to have one brand on it. Mine."

Webb's wonder left him immediately, as he turned to look closely at Holichek. "How can you do that? These brushpoppers are starving. They won't make enough to last till next year on what you pay for their beef. Half of them will go under. Bandine's the biggest one in the brush and he's only got a fifty-fifty chance of staying in the saddle. If the New Orleans market drops even a dollar, he might lose his shirt. . . ."

"And if one man in this brush gets wind of what's up, we won't make a cent," Holichek said. He squeezed Webb's arm again. "You have a chance to make more money than you ever made before in your life, Webb." His voice grew husky. "Do you really care what happens to the brushpoppers?"

Webb settled slowly into his chair. All the youth seeped out of his face, leaving a sunken look to his cheeks. He smiled, as if to himself, and his eyes had a pale shine.

"No," he said. "I don't care what happens to them."

After the boy had left, Holichek put his elbows on the table and leaned heavily against them. Why had he been such a fool? He could have used the boy as a buyer without letting him know where the cattle were headed. Just had to show somebody how big he was, didn't he? Couldn't stand to sit back and see Big Bob have the limelight. Just had to pop off with a lot of bull like he was the only one who could tell them the real inside, make them think he was the President of the U.S. or something. He had lost the Butterfield contract the same way. Somebody had kept prodding him about how important Big Bob was and comparing his deals with Big Bob's and finally he'd pulled the cork and told them, when it should have been kept quiet, just to see their eyes bug out.

It always seemed to come after Bob's visits. He recognized it as a reaction to the sense of inferiority Bob always instilled in him, a compensation for being shoved aside like an old shoe while the great man was in town. But it didn't help any to recognize it. He had made a fool of himself again, and he would be damned lucky if he didn't lose this one, too.

VIII

Webb did more riding during that spring and summer than he had ever done before. But his contract with Dan Holichek called for $500 when the cattle were sold, and that much money in such a desperate time would make a man rich. Webb was surprised to find that he actually began to enjoy the easy, outdoor life, the position of authority without too much responsibility attached. All he had to do was buy the cattle and let the seller worry about delivery. And he was popular enough in the lonely cow camps with his news from the outside, his casual ease with men, his skill at cards.

To keep Holichek's name out of it, Webb told his family he was acting as agent for an Eastern firm of speculators. They weren't too keen about it, but thought that anything was better than hanging around the saloon in town. And the life had touched off something else in Webb; it had brought to the surface a restlessness that was to characterize him deeply in later life. He knew that when the gather was over, he would have to return to the empty, listless days in town. He found the thought almost unbearable. It was what made him begin toying with the idea of traveling north with the herd. Claire didn't want him to, but the major wrote from Austin that it might make a man of him.

Holichek had gathered his cattle in half a dozen spots widely scattered through the brush. Each herd had a separate crew and none of the men in any one crew knew their connection with the other crews. Only the trail bosses knew their destination, and they were sworn to secrecy. The herds were to move out separately, in different directions, not turning north or hitting one trail till far beyond San Antonio. Webb was to work in Garrison's crew, and on the day he was to leave word came out of the brush about Bandine.

Everyone had expected the man to head for New Orleans again. But it was said that he meant to drive for Sedalia. That amused Holichek hugely. Three other big drovers had tried to reach the Chicago markets earlier that spring by driving to Sedalia. They had been cut to pieces by bushwhackers and Indians and the Kansas farmers, who had armed and organized to prevent the cattle coming through, afraid of the dread Texas fever being introduced to their own stock. The cattlemen had lost every head of beef and had been lucky to get back alive.

It all meant little to Webb, who joined Garrison at Benavides and started off on what was to be the big adventure. From there on out it was twelve and fourteen hours a day in the saddle and another two or three night hawking. It was dust and heat and stampedes and hunger and bitter exhaustion. The only thing that kept him from quitting was the fact that he didn't have a dime and knew he could never find his way back across the endless prairies alone. He was almost glad for what then happened at Fort Worth.

When he returned to Spanish Crossing, afterward, he didn't say anything about the incident or tell how he got the fare to ride the stagecoach back. He was still weak and pale from the wound he'd received, and everybody assumed that he had simply lacked what it took to stick it out. Webb was still a little worried about what he had said at Fort Worth to Bandine, but as time went on and nothing came of it, he, too, forgot. He found himself gravitating to the saloon again. He had made the acquaintance of a professional gambler in Fort Worth, while convalescing from his wound, and had picked up a lot from the man. When O'Hara saw his improvement, he invited the youth to become a house dealer. It amused Webb at first. But it did something to his vanity, too. So he took the job.

He had a fight with the major about it and moved to town. After that came the girl named Rosita, from Martinez Alley, with the smooth shoulders and the red lips. She had been Garrison's girl, but the man was gone now. So she was there, that October night, with an early frost lying like a silver crust on the town, and the kerosene lamps spitting and flaring in the drafty *cantina*. Webb was dealing for a group made up of Ewing Samuels, Jerry Waggoner, Dan Holichek, and Hammond Innes, one of the cattlemen who had lost his herd driving to Sedalia. It had been a close game, and they were all intent upon their cards when the brittle creak of rigging and the stamp and snort of many horses came from the street. In a moment the door was thrust open and a man came in, so tall that he had to stoop deeply to get through the opening. Innes was the first to turn, then he shoved his chair back with a shriek and jumped to his feet.

"Bandine. It's Bandine. And look what he drug in with him."

As Innes ran to the man, pumping his hand and clapping him on the back and shouting joyfully, the rest of them came in. Chico Morales and the Graves brothers and three or four more Bandine had taken north with him. O'Hara immediately began setting up drinks for them, and Bandine turned to him with a broad grin.

"Only one, O'Hara. I haven't seen my kids in so long I've forgot what they look like. We just stopped in for a bracer to get us the rest of the way."

He shoved his hat back on his head, rumpling his hand through hair that had grown long and wolfish about his ears, curling in a mane down the back of his neck. There was the drawn look of deep weariness to his face; a red beard covered his gaunt jaw, curly and matted as mesquite grass.

"You look pretty happy for a man that lost his herd to them Sedalia bushwhackers," Holichek said.

Bandine squinted against the raw fire of the whiskey, then let his breath out with a sound like steam escaping from an engine.

"No Sedalia bushwhackers that far west, Holichek." Webb saw Holichek's eyes grow narrow, and felt a sudden apprehension run through him. Even he had assumed that Bandine was back too early to have made a successful drive. It had to be that way, it had to be.

Bandine downed his second drink, winking at Webb. "See you got a new gal, kid. Even prettier'n the one at Fort Worth."

"You didn't see him at Fort Worth," Holichek snapped.

"How do you think he got back here?" Chico grinned. "Nobody else was going to take care of that knife wound."

Holichek's massive head turned slowly to Webb. "You didn't tell me you had a fight."

Webb absently riffled the deck of cards, his eyes fixed doggedly on them. "Some woman faro dealer. Her boyfriend didn't like the way I was making eyes at her or something. He had a knife."

"He makes it sound like a tea party," Chico said. The liquor was affecting him now; his eyes were glowing brightly and his lips were slack and damp. "Webb would have died if we hadn't been coming through that same night. We heard about it in another saloon and went looking for the kid."

"Never mind, Chico," Bandine said.

"Why not? It's just like Webb not to give you any credit," Chico said. He turned back to Holichek. "Bandine held the herd up till he was sure Webb would be all right. He even gave him the fare home."

"And him a Republican!" Bandine laughed. He emptied another drink and exhaled huskily. His voice sounded slurred and his grin was growing tipsy. "We ain't had nothing to eat

90

since morning. Another shot like that and I'll be too drunk to go home."

Webb pulled his chair back, trying to sound casual. "I'll see you later."

Before he could rise, Holichek grasped his arm, pinning it to the table. The man's fingers pinched so tightly that Webb winced in pain and started to struggle. But he could not tear free before Holichek asked Bandine: "You didn't drive to Sedalia?"

"Hell, no. Think we'd go there after we heard about Abilene?"

Webb quit struggling, abruptly, because he knew it was all over then. Holichek slowly turned to him, still gripping his arm. The blood had drained from the man's swarthy cheeks till the parchment color of them stood out in sharp contrast to his jet black beard. Bandine saw the expression and blinked his eyes, as if trying to concentrate through a drunken befuddlement.

"Holichek," he said. "I thought you knew. . . ." He stared at Webb, shaking his head, trying to clear it. "Kid, I didn't realize. . . ."

Holichek's grip on Webb's arm tightened till pain contracted the muscles. "You told him about Abilene," he said hoarsely.

Webb was gripping the cards in his free hand so tightly they bent almost double. "What did you expect?" he said in a brittle defiance. "What did I owe you? Garrison left me there to die. Didn't stay an extra five minutes to get me a doctor. . . ."

Holichek cut him off with a strangled sound of rage, as if unable to contain himself longer. He jumped up, sweeping his chair back with one hand so hard it skittered across the room and smashed against the bar. He caught Webb by both lapels and hauled him bodily out of the chair, and then jerked one hand back to smash Webb in the face.

"Holichek!" Bandine bawled.

Webb did not think he had ever heard anyone shout so loud. It halted Holichek. Still holding Webb up on his toes by the grip on his coat, still holding his fist back to strike, the man sent a sidelong glance toward Bandine. Webb could see it, too. Bandine had his gun out, pointed at Holichek.

"Let him go," Bandine said. He was swaying a little on his feet, from the drink. It seemed forever till Holichek's grip on Webb's coat relaxed, letting him sink back onto his heels. "Step back," Bandine said. Again that measureless space of time, before Holichek complied. He glared at Webb for a long time, wheezing a little with the constriction of his rage. Finally he turned to Bandine.

"What happened?" he said thickly.

"You won't like it," Bandine told him.

"What happened?"

"We beat you to Abilene, Holichek. After Webb told me, I left word for the other trail drivers that were coming through Fort Worth. They followed me and we found a Seminole that showed us a short cut across the Canadian, and we beat Garrison. By the time he got there, the first train was already loaded and the pens were full. Garrison had to hold all his herds on the prairie and a summer thunderstorm stampeded 'em. Time he got 'em all gathered up, he'd lost half the beef. He didn't want to risk that again by holding 'em in the open. But he knew the men that were already in the pens had first call on the next train, so he tried to beat 'em by driving his cattle east and meeting the train before it hit Abilene. Bushwhackers caught him on the river and cut him to pieces."

Holichek had watched Bandine with wide, blank eyes all the time he was speaking. He spoke through clenched teeth. "You're lying," he said.

"Garrison should be back pretty soon. He'll tell you the same thing."

Holichek's eyes dropped to the gun in Bandine's hand. Webb saw little muscles bunch and knot in his swarthy jowls, and thought for a moment that the threat of the gun wouldn't be enough. Finally, however, the man hauled about to look at Webb. His voice had lowered, though it still had that wheezing sound, till it was barely audible. "Kid," he said, "you'd better get out of town tonight. If I ever see you again, I think I'll kill you."

Webb stared emptily at the man. He could see the rage dancing through Holichek's eyes and knew that he meant what he said. But it drew little fear from Webb. There seemed no capacity for emotion left in him. Grayly he put the cards down and turned to walk outside. He halted on the curb, in the pitch-black shadow of the overhang, shivering a little in the chill, feeling the let-down in him. It was always this way after violence, after failure.

He felt no sense of betrayal at having told Bandine about Abilene; he never had felt it, even at the time. He had been delirious with his wound then, and bitter against Garrison for leaving him to die, and had babbled the whole thing to Bandine in a violent need to strike back at Garrison any way he could. After Bandine had left and Webb had a clearer conception of what he had done, he did not worry too much. For even if Bandine headed for Abilene, Webb had never dreamed he could beat Garrison. But now it was done, the whole thing, ending as so many other things had ended in his life, muddily, ignominiously. He couldn't even feel his failure very keenly.

He heard the walk shudder beneath the clatter of boots as Bandine and the others came out behind him. He turned and said dully to Bandine: "I suppose I should thank you again."

Bandine's grin was slack and a little silly with drink. "Never mind, kid. You'd just better leave town. Holichek's really fit to kill you. I may've gone soft twice, but I just couldn't save a Republican three times in a row."

IX

Despite the political strife that marked the last months of 1867, the cattle business boomed. Almost thirty-five thousand steers had been shipped out of Abilene that fall, and Eastern quotations were zooming. Winter was not ordinarily a time of roundup, but cattle fever gripped the brush, and it was overrun with maverickers. They were a wild bunch, mostly troops just returned from a war to find themselves faced with joblessness and starvation. In their fight for survival they made little distinction between private and public lands, and the big ranchers were hard put to defend their thickets. Still, Bandine realized that a man who owned his land would eventually be the winner. In the first place, he would not be subject to the competition of the hundreds of maverickers who were cutting the profits so thin in a free graze. He had the right to exclude them from his pastures, if he had the strength to back it up. So Bandine spent that winter using the money he had made at Abilene to buy land and build his crew.

He tried to make Chico a partner, but the youth did not want the responsibility. So he took him on as foreman and gave him the job of hiring. That left Bandine free to spend the countless days riding the holdings of prospective sellers, flushing the mavericks, and estimating how many head the areas held. He bought land from a Mexican whose title came down from the original grant given by the King of Spain; he bought land from families who had colonized it under contracts with the Mexican government. He bought four thousand six hundred and five acres from a woman who had got it as a donation grant for a grandfather who had died in the Texas Revolution. He bought three hundred and twenty acres from a homesteader who had qualified for pre-emption patents. He spent all of October away from home and didn't get back till well into November.

It was dusk when he returned that second time, with the

brush lying in feathery masses all about him. It was cold and he was huddled into his canvas Mackinaw, slack with the weariness of endless riding, endless haggling. He heard the piping voices of his kids before he reached open ground.

"I shot you, you gotta lie down and be dead."

"You can't kill me. I'm Grampa Willoughby and I grinned all your fingers off before you even pulled the trigger."

Bandine broke free of the brush to see Rusty running down a corral fence, dragging Bandine's rusty Civil War Springfield after him. It was longer than the boy and almost threw him off his feet, rattling and thumping along the ground. He saw Bandine and stopped by a fence post, staring owl-eyed at the man. There was a rustle in the brush, as Bandine swung off his horse, and Kit appeared, creeping out of the thicket on her hands and knees. Her face was scratched and her long yellow hair was matted with brambles and full of mesquite berries. Bandine stood grinning at them, waiting beside his horse for Kit's rush. But neither child moved.

"Ain't you gonna say hello?" he asked.

"Daddy?" Kit asked.

It was more a rhetorical question, for she obviously recognized him. He frowned at their strange hesitance. "Sure it's Daddy, what's the matter with you kids?"

Kit got to her feet and came slowly toward him, a thumb in her mouth. But when he bent toward her and held out his arms she finally began to run toward him. Still she did not squeal the way she always had as he scooped her up. He was used to Rusty's shyness, but it was something new in Kit. He felt how heavy she was becoming, and realized she was five years old. Was it merely a phase in growing up? He looked at Rusty again, seeing that the boy still hung back, leaning to one side and peering around Bandine as if to see something behind him. Thinking it was merely a childish artifice, Bandine squatted down, still holding Kit in one arm, and grinned broadly at the boy.

"Ain't you the quiet one. Tell me what you been doing, now. How many Injuns you shot today?"

"Didn't shoot any."

Bandine couldn't help frowning again. He had ceased trying to fathom Rusty's strange, withdrawn nature, but it seemed more intensely reserved than ever, the freckled face almost stony in its expression.

"How about a ride, then? You ain't topped that bronc' in a long time."

"Don't want no ride."

Bandine straightened up again, shaking his head helplessly, and turned to go inside, twining his fingers in Kit's silken hair. It was yellow as corn tassel. She was getting to look more like her mother every day. It sent a momentary streak of melancholy through him, to have Catherine recalled so vividly, as he pushed open the door, stooping through. Adah was bent over the grate, stirring something in a pot, and turned to greet him with more enthusiasm than her usual reserve allowed. He sniffed appreciatively of the cooking syrup.

"You know what that is, Kit? That's prickly-pear candy, so sticky you take one bite and can't get your teeth apart."

Rusty moved through the door behind them, placing himself ceremoniously against the wall. "Don't like prickly-pear candy," he announced.

Bandine sent an oblique glance toward him, then set Kit on the table. "What's wrong with these kids, Adah?"

The gladness left her face. "Man don't get home much, maybe he seems like a stranger."

He shrugged irritably out of his Mackinaw. "I've got to buy this land now or I'll never get it. With beef booming, land that goes for ten cents an acre this year will be three and four dollars next year."

"So you'll be rich. Maybe kids need a little more than money."

Bandine turned to Rusty. "What's got into all of you?"

Adah's cheeks sucked in angrily. "I guess I'd sulk, too, my pa forgot my birthday."

Bandine stared blankly at Adah. Then it exploded from him. "It is. It's the tenth. No wonder he was acting so strange. I've been running around like a cow with heel flies. Could have been Christmas and I wouldn't have known it." Bandine wheeled and took three tremendous strides across the room, dropping on one knee before Rusty and grasping his thin shoulders.

"Jigger, I plumb forgot. You got to tan my britches or something. How can I make it up to you? Let's go into town right now. . . ."

"Emery," protested Adah, "it'd be after midnight."

"We'll make Ewing Samuels open up that gol'-dang' store if it's three in the morning. We'll buy everything in the place. Red-topped boots and city-slicker pants and a buckskin shirt with fringe a mile long. . . ."

"Red-topped boots?" Rusty said solemnly.

Bandine could see it working through his head, and laughed huskily. "Sure thing. But a man don't wear boots 'less he tops that bronc'. How about it?"

"Red-topped boots," the boy repeated soberly.

He was not smiling yet, but his eyes had begun to glow. Bandine got down on his hands and knees, coaxing the boy to climb on. Rusty regarded him with a solemn stare. But Bandine saw the flush of excitement begin to stain his freckled cheeks, and began crow-hopping around the room. Finally Rusty could contain himself no longer.

"Red-topped boots!" he shouted, and ran and scrambled on

Bandine's back.

Kit squealed and ran after him and climbed on, too, and Bandine began pitching around the room on his hands and knees like a wild horse, with both of them shouting and hollering and pulling his shaggy hair in an effort to stay on, and, when he looked up to Adah, he saw that she was smiling and there were tears in her eyes.

They were making so much noise that Bandine didn't hear the knock on the door. He saw Adah walk to it and open it. Chico Morales stood there, rubbing his hands to take the chill out of them. The intense, burning look of his eyes made his face look thin and drawn. That always came when there was trouble, and it caused Bandine to stop the horseplay immediately.

"We found a couple of mavericks in Wolf Sink burned with the Double Sickle," Chico said. "The brand was so fresh the hair still smelled. You told me to let you know."

Bandine saw a brittle light come into Adah's eyes. He knew what she was thinking. He stared at the wall a long time before he could force himself to turn and face Rusty.

"I got to go, jigger. It won't do us any good to get any land if we can't keep the mavericks off. They cleaned out some of Innes's biggest thickets last month. He said, if it keeps up, he'll be out of business. If we don't stop them now, we might as well quit."

There was no accusation in the boy's eyes, not even hurt. But the glow left them like a snuffed candle. They grew dark and solemn. Although he didn't move a muscle, it was as if he had slowly withdrawn himself, till he was completely out of Bandine's reach. Torn between the two forces pulling at him, Bandine sent an intensely helpless glance at Adah.

"I suppose you're right," she said. "You got to go." Then a bitter thinness came to her voice. "You might make your kids rich, Emery, but you're goin' to lose them doing it."

Major Nadell was in Spanish Crossing the morning Bandine brought in the maverickers. Nadell always stayed at the inn during the week, when court was in session. His appointment to the bench had come during the summer, when General Sheridan deposed the Supreme Court justices and many of the district judges who had any taint of Secessionist connections. Nadell knew a deep desire to see Texas back on its feet, but his experience as a military commander of Spanish Crossing had been a disappointing one, and he felt he would be more qualified to aid the Reconstruction in a judicial capacity. Thus he had been only too glad to resign his commission and accept appointment to the Spanish Crossing district.

There was a lot of land litigation starting, and his eyes ached from a late study of briefs the night before. But his mind was not upon that, as he stood before the mirror, shaving himself. He was thinking of his son.

He was still not over the shock of the boy's departure. When he had finally found out its cause, he had gone directly to Holichek. The man had talked freely of it, openly admitting his plan to corner the Abilene beef shipment for that year. Nadell's first impulse had been to condemn him for it. But Ewing Samuels and Jerry Waggoner had not seemed particularly shocked, and it made Nadell realize that to a businessman it was probably merely a sharp deal. Holichek also admitted having threatened Webb for wrecking his plan, but he seemed cooled off now.

What hurt Nadell worst was that Webb had not come to him about it, had left town that night without even returning home. The boy had written from El Paso, only touching on his reasons for leaving. Nadell had answered immediately, asking him to return, telling him that Holichek was over his anger. But Webb had not responded. Aside from a poignant hurt, it left Nadell with a feeling that had come to him more obscurely before, in connection with Webb—a sense of some dark side to the boy that he would never understand and with which he was totally inadequate to cope.

He was sunk so deep in his reflections that a knock on the door made him nick himself. Holding his finger to the cut, he walked to open the door. It was Claire, in her dark green cloak, the chill bringing a high color to her cheeks and causing her eyes to sparkle.

"I thought I'd shop today and started early," she said, stepping in to give him a kiss on his cheek. "Have you heard about Bandine?"

"What now?"

"He's down in front of court with two men he claims are rustlers. He won't turn them over to Sheriff Geddings. He wants a trial right away."

Nadell frowned. "I can't do it. My docket is full for today."

"I knew that's what he'd run up against. An argument has already started down there, Dad. The sheriff has sent for Captain Prevent. I know Bandine won't give in to him, either. You remember what happened the last time Bandine was brought in. If the people try to help him again, the lid might blow off. Things are bad enough with this new military occupation. Can't you make an exception of this case?"

Nadell shook his head helplessly. "Am I forever doomed to have Emery Bandine breathing down the back of my neck?"

He sent her down to get the bailiff and to inform Bandine, while he finished shaving. Then he put on his coat and went to the courthouse. Bandine was not in sight but there was a sullen look to the little knots of men who had gathered all along the sidewalks. Sheriff Geddings and Captain Prevent were in the courtroom with Bandine, Chico Morales, the bailiff, and two brushpoppers. One was a Mexican Nadell did not recognize but he saw that the other was Henry Tevis, a man who had spent some time around town in the company of Dan Holichek and Charlie Garrison.

Nadell waved aside the bailiff's announcement and took his seat. "I see that a warrant has been prepared. I'll hear your complaint, Bandine."

Bandine came forward, towering above the others, looking a little older to Nadell, a little more weathered. Though many men were adopting the new Petnecky spurs, he still wore the great Mexican cartwheels that filled the room with their clatter as he walked. He told Nadell that he and Chico had captured the two men red-handed in Wolf Sink Thickets. Tevis claimed he didn't know he'd crossed the line into Wolf Sink Thickets. Nadell asked Bandine if he had any proof of the rustling. Bandine said they had a dozen cows out in the brush. Were the brands blotted? No. Then why did he say they were rustling?

"They were gathering beef on my land. What else is that if it ain't rustling?"

"Mavericking," Tevis said. "We was just mavericking."

"If you have no proof of an altered brand, and the cattle were all over a year old and had only Tevis's brand on them, the only charge you can bring against them is one of trespassing," Nadell said.

Bandine exploded. "If you had a Secessionist up here, I bet my boots it would be rustling. You'd give him ten years. . . ."

Nadell banged his gavel until Bandine ceased. "If you don't show more respect for the court, Bandine, I'll have to find you in contempt. There's no law against mavericking. . . ."

"Damn you, Major, you're just trying to twist this up. You know the mavericks will put us out of business if we don't stop them somehow. Maybe that's what you carpetbaggers want. Be too bad to have a damned Secesh cattleman get too rich and powerful, wouldn't it?"

"I find you in contempt, Bandine. That will be fifty dollars."

"It won't stop me, Judge. If we can't get satisfaction in our own courts, we'll take it into our own hands. You'll have a bigger war on your hands than. . . ."

Nadell banged his gavel again, filling the room with its echoes, until Bandine finally stopped. Nadell felt the nausea of deep anger churning through him. Why did Bandine always draw it from him? Was it his own sense of inadequacy before the man's violence? He leaned toward Bandine, his words coming in short breathless gusts, the way they always did when he was struggling to suppress his anger.

"In my eyes there is no such thing as a Unionist or a Secessionist. That was over and done with years ago. I am here to interpret the laws as they now stand. I am not going to let the fact that a man is the richest rancher in the county make me twist those laws to his benefit. You have no proof that these men were rustling. If you want to prefer charges of trespassing against them, I will fine them twenty dollars."

"Trespass, hell . . . !"

"And the next time I find you in contempt, I will not resort to fine. There is an old charge against you. Failure to apply for parole. Refusal to surrender property. Texas is a military district again, you know. That could well mean you'd be sent to Huntsville."

There was an aching silence in the room. Bandine's jaws were clamped so tightly little bulges of muscle leaped and jumped down their bony edge. Then, without a word, he wheeled and stalked out, his spurs clattering like a cavalry charge.

Claire had watched the proceedings from behind the rail that separated the audience seats from the jury box. She saw how blank Bandine's eyes were, how pale and set his face was, as he swung through the gate and headed for the hall that led outside.

She knew the depths of his rages, and felt a sudden fear of what he might do now. She followed him swiftly, catching him halfway down the hall, grasping his arm.

"Emery, what are you going to do?"

"I don't know. I got to blow my lid somehow. I'm going to get drunk and I'm going to bust this town apart."

"And land yourself right in jail," she said.

"I can't help it. If I don't get drunk, I'll come apart at the seams. I'll go back in there and kill those rustlers. . . ."

"But the town is under military jurisdiction, Emery. You get drunk and cause trouble and they'll send you to Huntsville for sure. Dad won't even have a chance to intervene. A year is the least you'll get. Will you let your kids in for something like that?"

It was the only thing that could have reached him. He stared down at her, shaking his head, opening his mouth to speak, then closing it again. She pulled him gently toward one of the rooms that opened off the hall, not wanting him to be out on the street till he was cooled off. She shut the door behind her and leaned against it. In a moment she heard the tramp of boots pass down the hall and knew it was Tevis and the others leaving. She saw Bandine's hands clamp shut, saw a white ridge appear about his compressed lips. But he made no move toward the door. He stood with his great shoulders a little stooped, staring at the floor, the breath passing huskily through him. She knew now what Adah had meant when she said the depth of Bandine's feelings frightened her sometimes. Finally he turned to look at Claire.

"I don't know why I let a little Unionist like you do that to me."

"Can't you stop thinking in those terms, Emery? The war's over. . . ."

"Carpetbaggers like your dad keep twisting the laws around

and it'll start all over again."

"But there's no law against mavericking."

As if seeking some release for his pent-up anger, he caught her by the elbows, shaking her. "It wasn't mavericking. They were rustling my cows on my land. Nobody's going to do that, Claire. I worked too hard to get that for my kids."

He stopped, breathing heavily. She saw the change run palpably through him; the focus of his eyes altered, as if he were realizing for the first time how close he had brought her. Close enough for her to feel the sudden tremor run through his body. She realized then how long he must have been without a woman, how much his pure physical need of one must be by now. And she saw that the feel of her in his hands had released that need.

"Emery," she said, "why must so many things stand between us, when there shouldn't be anything . . . ?"

Her head tipped back as she said it, and her eyes half closed. He made a sound deep in his throat and drew her to him. She met it fully with a passion of her own and did not know how long it lasted. Finally he took his lips off and held her away, staring down at her with a strange expression in his face. Even through the tumult of her own senses she realized that he had responded without thought to the deep and vital needs built up within him through the lonely years, and that only now was he realizing the full implications of it. He dropped her arms and stepped back, his voice trembling with anger.

"That would have been nice," he said, "if it hadn't been with a damn' carpetbagger."

X

For Rusty, those years passed swiftly, with but fleeting impressions of his father stamped upon his memory. During most of 1868 it was the new house. Every spare minute of Bandine's time seemed to be taken up with its building. Adah was more disgusted than pleased, saying, if it wasn't one thing to keep him away, it was another. But Bandine kept promising her that once this was finished he would have more time to himself. And then, on Christmas Day, they moved in.

It looked like a castle to Rusty, set up on the high land overlooking the river. The marble entrance hall was so highly polished that the boy could look down and see the inverted reflection of the towering red-headed giant carrying the two kids in his arms, the noisy clanking of his spurs echoing into the dark chasms of the house. Bandine carried them ceremoniously through all the rooms, grinning happily at Kit's gurgling fascination with the gold-threaded damask hangings, laughing outright as Rusty had to be lowered at each new piece of furniture to inspect the legs that had claws on them "just like lions and tigers."

The move was to mark more than one change in their life. The nearest public school was in Spanish Crossing, much too far away to attend, and Bandine finally gave in to Adah's urgings and hired a tutor from Kansas City. He was Mr. Dalhart, a shy, bookish introvert in his early forties who came to live at the house. He had a way, with his picture books and his stories, that somehow taught a boy how to make sums while he was hearing about bears and Indians and such.

But Bandine did not make good his promise to Adah. The trouble with the maverickers in the brush was growing more bitter, and took up more and more of his time. The first meeting was held at his house in the spring, with Hammond Innes and half a dozen other big cattlemen, and Jerry Waggoner, who had been their lawyer for years now. It was evening when they went to the library to talk, and Kit and Rusty crouched like nightgowned conspirators on the landing behind the railing, huddling closer together as the voices grew louder and angrier.

"I tell you, Jerry, we can't go on like this. Shoot a house-breaker and you wouldn't even be brought to trial. Shoot a man stealing your cattle and them carpetbag courts call it murder. I've sworn out a dozen complaints. The judge just says he can't hold the man because there's no law against mavericking."

"That's why we want you to run this year, Waggoner. If we can get a man down there to back this bill against maverick-ing. . . ."

"I wouldn't stand a chance in Austin, boys. One of the things Big Bob's bunch is most afraid of is a bill outlawing maverick-ing. The bulk of you big cattlemen are Democrats. As long as the mavericking goes on, it keeps you whittled down. As long as you're whittled down, you have no power to threaten Bob and his bunch if there's a gubernatorial election this year."

Before Kit and Rusty heard more that night they were caught by Adah and sent to bed. For countless evenings during that spring they lost their father to those smoke-filled meetings, and finally he left with Waggoner and Innes to campaign through the county in an effort to rally the big operators behind them. It was a lonely period for Rusty, in which he became more and more attached to the shy Mr. Dalhart. The man had an odd tal-ent for personalizing strange lands and exotic peoples; soon the Romans and the Greeks were as familiar to the kids as Chico and Adah; Rusty knew China and India better than he knew the back pastures.

Kit listened in rapt attention to Dalhart's stories but showed little inclination for study. It was Rusty who began to reveal a precocious hunger for reading, soon advancing far beyond the picture books and other simple primers of his age.

Toward the end of the year Bandine went down to Austin to seek more support for Waggoner. He was gone a couple of months, and the elections were held before his return. Wag-goner lost to Samuels, who had been sponsored by Bob Holi-

chek. It was only a small part of the whole radical victory, for
E.J. Davis had been elected governor, and one of the blackest
eras of Texas history was to begin.

Rusty was reading in the library that day his father returned
from Austin. Bandine appeared at the library door, carrying
Kit, trailed by Adah. He stopped there a moment, a haggard
look to his face, and seemed to gather a heartiness with some
effort.

"How's my boy?" he said. "Seems like you growed a foot
while I was gone."

Rusty got slowly to his feet, dark eyes fixed gravely on him.
As the man stalked over, Rusty had a vague sense of the weariness, the defeat lying in the grooves of his face. But Bandine
grinned at the boy, tousling his hair with one immense hand.
With his father standing so close, Rusty had to tip his head
back to keep the man's face in sight. It was like gazing up at
some Olympian god, and only increased the vague awe Bandine's immense size always inspired in Rusty. Yet, with that
hand tugging playfully at his hair, Rusty felt a warmth grow in
him, felt the impulse to react, to laugh as Kit did, to express
himself in some way. But it was a thing that formed slowly in
him, inhibited partly by the awe, partly by his own reserved
nature, perhaps even by an intuitive sense of the gap already
growing between him and his father.

Rusty took so long to respond that, before he could answer
the vague impulses in him, the grin faded from Bandine's face.
He turned away and walked to the chair, sitting down and putting Kit on his knee. Then he sent a darkly questioning glance
at Adah.

"You been gone too much, Emery," she said. "How many
times have I told you?"

"Is that all of it?" Bandine asked. "He ain't like me at all. He
ain't even like Catherine. Kit don't act that way."

"She ain't as old as Rusty. She's got more sunshine in her. But you keep this up and you'll lose her, too, Emery."

"And if I don't keep it up, I'll lose everything. . . ." Bandine broke off, as if realizing how angry he sounded. He lowered his head, running his hand through shaggy red hair. "I'm sorry, Adah. It just seems things are swarming on me from every side. With Davis and the radicals in, the maverickers will go wild. It'll be a regular war in the thickets, and I'll have to be out there fighting if I mean to hold any land at all. But I'm going to see my kids first. I swear I am." He looked up at Rusty, his face haggard and drawn. "It's horse day in town tomorrow. How about a new pony for you kids?"

A new pony? Rusty felt the thought take shape and work slowly through this mind, as new thoughts always did. It seemed he had thoroughly to explore and digest them before he could react to them. As Bandine saw his hesitation, he set Kit down and brought her over to Rusty, and knelt before them on one knee.

"I mean it this time, jigger," he said, grasping Rusty's arm. "Not like those red-top boots. Nothing will keep us from it. We'll go into town tomorrow."

The excitement did not really begin to work at Rusty till after they were put to bed. Then the darkness of his room came alive with high-stepping ponies—blacks and pintos and bays—with silver mountings in their saddles and crickets in their bits, and he tossed and turned till long after midnight, unable to sleep with the anticipation of it.

Horse day usually fell on Saturday, when people from the whole countryside drove into town to trade and buy animals and do their shopping. Claire Nadell joined the throng, driving the buckboard in to pick up her father at the inn and to lay in supplies for the coming week. It was a crisp and bright winter day, with the sun soon melting the patches of frost encrusting the ground. The main street was crowded with traffic of every sort. She had to wait five minutes to get past a snarl of buckboards and linch-pin wagons before the Martinez house. As she parked in front of the store, she saw a trio of blue-coated riders force their way roughly through the crowd around the horse trading. She realized they were members of the new state police formed by Governor Davis.

She was still watching them when she caught sight of Emery Bandine, coming down the sidewalk. He was flanked by his two kids, and Adah was behind him. Claire was surprised at how much the children had grown, and it made her realize how long it had been since she'd last seen them. Rusty was tall for his age, all arms and legs, gangling and awkward as a young colt. Kit commanded an immediate attention from everyone she passed, with her tumbling bright yellow hair and her enormous blue eyes.

But it was in Bandine, mostly, that Claire noticed change. The last few years of politics and mingling with the more sophisticated crowds in the larger cities had smoothed him down noticeably. He was wearing a gray fustian and mole-skin trousers instead of his usual brush clothes. The coat made his shoulders look enormously broad, but it took some of the wildness out of his towering figure. Claire saw his eyes focus on her as he came through the crowd—saw the smile start to form on his lips, then stop. She knew what he was thinking of, because it was in her mind, too.

It had been a long time since that kiss in the courthouse, but she had been unable to forget it. A man did not kiss a woman that way without a deep and vital need for her. And the desire it aroused in Claire had convinced her more than ever that Bandine was the only man for her. Yet, seeing the stiff politeness come to his face now, she was struck again with the deep sense of all the barriers that stood between them. It gave her a help-less feeling, made their conversation a stilted and prosaic camouflage for the feelings that stirred like smoke in their eyes.

Bandine removed his hat. "Good afternoon, ma'am."

"Hello, Emery. I haven't seen you with your children in so long that I'd forgotten you were a family man."

His face darkened a little. "I'm going to try and remedy that, ma'am."

There was an awkward moment, with both of them hanging on the brink of something, and the stirring clamor of the crowd about them. Then, with an effort, Claire said: "I'm sorry you lost down in Austin."

A faint flush came to his cheeks. "This Davis is drunk with power," he said. "Nobody's goin' to submit to the things he's started. If he tries to put those state police in Spanish Crossing, he'll find he has a bull by the tail. . . ."

She put a hand on his arm. "Emery, not so loud. They're already here. Talk like that will only antagonize them. The maverick trouble has already given this town a bad reputation. They're just waiting to make an example of somebody."

As Claire finished speaking, three men came into view, push-ing through the crowd from O'Hara's across the street. Claire saw that Dan Holichek was walking between Henry Tevis and Charlie Garrison. Holichek had a hand on each man's shoulder, the inevitable black cigar between his teeth. There was a swag-ger to their walk, a flush to their faces that told her they had all been drinking. With exaggerated courtesy, they all removed their hats to Claire, in greeting. Then Holichek turned to Ban-dine.

"Didn't think the Democrats would have the stomach for town today, Emery. Some of the boys have a trough of mud in front of O'Hara's. Claim it's for any of your crowd that shows up."

"Emery," Adah said sharply. "The kids. . . ."

"Don't worry, Miss Adah." Holichek chuckled. "I don't run with that rough bunch. I figure a man knows when he's been beaten."

"And how he's been beaten," Bandine said thinly. "Waggoner thought that as long as the maverickers kept us big operators whittled down, we wouldn't have the power to buck Big Bob in Austin."

An alcoholic slyness filled Holichek's eyes. "Seemed to work out that way."

"Maybe you did some of the whittling," Bandine said.

Holichek allowed a look of mock hurt to raise his brows and pout his lips. Claire saw Bandine flush, and realized how it must have goaded him. She knew how long the maverick trouble had prodded him, knew what added pressures the recent defeat at the polls must have built up in him. She wondered suddenly how much riding he could take. Knowing his capacity for violence when he could no longer contain himself, she tried to avert it.

"What does it matter?" she asked. "It's over now. Emery, take me to the horse trading."

He did not seem to hear her. He was staring at Holichek, and spoke in a brittle voice. "I saw a big herd on my way north last year. Trail boss was running half a dozen different bunches under his road brand. I estimated three or four hundred of your Scissors H."

"Lots of free brush left."

"I hope that's where you got those cattle. If I find a Scissors H in my pastures. . . ."

"There still ain't no law against mavericking."

Bandine flushed deeply. Then the expression changed, as if before a new realization, and he asked roughly: "Were you in Wolf Sink again?"

Claire saw that Holichek was just drunk enough to relish prodding Bandine. He tapped ash from his cigar, grinning impishly at Garrison. "I don't rightly recall. Were we in Wolf Sink, Charlie?"

Bandine's big hands closed into knobby fists. Claire realized how far they had driven him and caught his arm. "Emery. . . ."

He shook her off. "Give me a straight answer, Holichek. If you got those steers in Wolf Sink. . . ."

"What would you do?" Holichek's voice was abruptly contemptuous. "Haul us in for trespassing?"

Both Tevis and Garrison burst out laughing. With a savage grunt, Bandine caught Holichek by both his lapels and jammed him back against the two-by-four support of the overhang.

"Damn you, Holichek, I told Garrison what I'd do the next time I found you in my pastures. Do I have to break you up to keep you out of there?"

Holichek reacted with an anger of his own, taking that moment to regain his balance and then lunging back into Bandine, striking viciously at his belly. It knocked Bandine back, and Holichek tried to follow it up. Doubled over, with all the air knocked from him, Bandine still managed to block the second blow and throw himself against Holichek. It caught the man off balance and sent him stumbling backward to trip off the curb and fall flat on his back in the street.

Claire saw a blue-coated rider come into view from Third, staring at the commotion. She tried to warn Bandine, but Garrison was already running into him from behind. Bandine was knocked off the curb after Holichek, driving him to his hands and knees in the street. Garrison jumped off and tried to hit the back of his neck before he came up.

But Bandine switched around and lunged into the man belly-high, arms flailing around his waist. As Garrison staggered backward toward the crowd, Tevis jumped at Bandine from the other side. For a moment it was all a wild scuffle of kicking arms and legs.

Then Tevis stumbled free and sat down hard, hugging his belly, an ashen look to his face. It left Bandine grappling with Garrison, right up against the crowd of onlookers. At the same time Claire saw that Holichek had regained his feet and was rushing Bandine.

Claire cried a warning and Bandine flung Garrison from him to wheel around. When he saw Holichek coming at him, he lunged to meet the man. Before they reached one another, the shouting crowd parted before a blue-coated rider who ran his horse between Bandine and Holichek. Bandine was rushing so hard he ran against the horse. He pushed away from it with a grunt, looking up in surprised anger, and then tried to veer around its head. But another rider came in behind Bandine, leaned out of the saddle, and hit him across the back of the neck with a six-shooter.

Claire felt a horrified gasp leave her as it drove Bandine against the first horse again, where he sagged for a second, then dropped to his hands and knees on the ground. She tried to reach him, but the packed crowd cut her off. Tevis was on his feet now, still holding his belly. He joined Garrison and Holichek where they stood above Bandine, staring down at him. The sound of their breathing rose gustily above the other babble.

A third blue-coated policeman had ridden up and was stepping off his horse. He was a thick-bodied man, black-browed, unshaven.

"What's the trouble, Mister Holichek?"

Holichek shook his head helplessly. "I don't rightly know, Captain. We were just walking over to see the horse trading. Stopped to pass the time of day with Bandine here. He started threatening me about mavericking. Grabbed me, almost tore my coat off. The crowd'll vouch for that."

The captain glanced around, his face growing more truculent at the assent from half a dozen men in the street. Then he toed Bandine. "You better get up, mister. I heard about you. We got a place for unreconstructed Rebs."

Bandine was still dazed and got to his feet with difficulty. He held the back of his neck, eyes squinted in pain. Claire had fought through the crowd by then, and confronted the captain.

"Holichek wasn't giving you a true picture. They were goading Bandine. . . ."

"It'll all come out in court, ma'am," the captain said. A humorless smile broke over his face. "He'll only get ten years or so."

Bandine was too dazed to struggle as the captain caught his arm and shoved him southward on the street, the two mounted men clearing the way. Claire started to follow, then remembered the children on the sidewalk. Confused and frightened, Kit had begun to cry.

"Where's my pony? Daddy promised he'd get me a pony. . . ."

Adah pulled the little girl against her skirts. "Hush, Kit. You'll be lucky to see your daddy again, much less a pony."

XI

Bandine got off that time with a fine and a warning to stay out of town for a week. It was Nadell's leniency that saved him. The police tried to press the issue and have him jailed, but they could find no charge that would suffice for the judge. Bandine had no cause to go into town for the next months, being completely occupied with the calf roundup. He was coming to realize that he had overextended himself, paying out so much money for land in the prior years. With the enormously raised tax rate imposed by the Davis regime and the inroads made by the maverickers, Bandine found that the receipts of the trail herd barely met his obligations. A drop in the beef market or another big loss to maverickers could ruin him.

Already opposition was beginning to form against the excesses of the Davis regime, and the cattlemen grabbed at that straw as a last chance to get passed some legislative measure against mavericking. Bandine found himself involved in politics more and more. In September of 1871 he was chosen delegate to the Austin convention protesting the collection of illegal taxes by Davis. The Democrats managed to get Waggoner in that year, and Waggoner immediately introduced the bill to outlaw mavericking, but Big Bob still had enough power to hang it up in committee.

That was in February, with the panic already beginning to grow in the East. Most of the cattlemen thought it would die out, but Bandine was in no position to take a chance. He knew that, if the panic spread, the bottom would drop out of the beef market and he'd be ruined. He told Waggoner he'd have to give up the maverick bill for the present and get back to his spring roundup, making it a beef gather instead of a calf count. He returned in April to find that Chico had already gathered the roundup crews. Again he was struck by how much the children had grown and how little he had seen them during the hectic years of battling the Davis machine. He realized that the only way he'd get to see his kids at all for another three or four months was to have Rusty go on roundup with him. Adah thought the boy was still a little young, but Rusty was already half a foot taller than most boys his age, and Bandine said it was time he started learning the business. Rusty showed a strange reluctance to go, but Bandine was used to his reserve, and insisted. His only regret was that Kit couldn't go, too, but a cow camp was no place for a girl her age.

They made their main camp on the north fringe of Wolf Sink Thickets. It had taken most of the day to reach the thickets and the men began to turn in early. Rusty sat brooding by the fire, showing none of the excitement Bandine would normally expect from a boy on his first roundup. Rolling a cigarette by the chuck wagon, Bandine knew this was the moment he had waited for, if he'd really brought the boy along in the hope to get close to him again. But he felt oddly awkward, as if approaching a stranger. It was a distinct effort to go over and sit down on a saddle beside him.

"The brush won't be so scary, after a few days. You'll even get so you don't mind them thorns jabbing your hide. You just forgot how it was, jigger. Been spending too much time with Dalhart and them books."

"There's nothing wrong with Mister Dalhart."

Bandine saw the boyish irritation darken Rusty's face, knew he had made a mistake. "I didn't say there was, jigger. But the time's coming when you'll have to put the books aside and learn the cattle business."

"Put the books aside?" Rusty had turned toward Bandine, his eyes wide and almost frightened.

Bandine realized he'd made another mistake, and shook his head. "I don't mean for good. Cattleman's got all winter to read." He stopped, seeing Rusty was unconvinced. He thought maybe he'd started out on the wrong trail. Maybe begin with what interested Rusty, and then lead into the cattle business. That made him realize how little he knew of the boy's interests. "Funny. That Dalhart's been around the house a long time. I never really knew what he was teaching you."

"Arithmetic. History."

"What kind of history?"

"He gives me books about the Greeks now."

"I knew a Greek once. He tried to run an outfit down along the Brazos. . . ."

"Not that kind of Greek. Two thousand years ago."

"Oh."

Bandine felt stupid. Then one of the men stirred in his blankets and it made Bandine realize that everyone in the crew was probably listening. He knew an intense embarrassment that they should hear his inability to reach his son. It blocked him from trying again.

"You better roll in," he said lamely. "Up before dawn tomorrow."

Wanting to escape the pressure of the listening crew, he walked miserably out into the brush. He stood in the darkness, trying to clear his thoughts. After a moment Chico joined him.

Seeing the sympathetic grin on the Mexican's face, Bandine asked: "What is it, Chico? I can't seem to touch him any more."

"Perhaps you try too hard, my friend. You must remember this. He is a boy, and you are a man. Until he grows up, no matter how close you grow to him otherwise, that gap will always stand between you. I love my father as few sons do. Yet I understand him a hundred times better now than I did at ten."

Bandine glanced at the man, feeling that Chico had touched a part of it. Yet that wasn't all, and he suddenly knew the same embarrassment he had felt with the listening crew. He looked away, voicing the first thought that came to his mind in an attempt to change the subject. "I wonder how big that panic will get?"

"Can't you forget that just one day? How can you get near your boy when you let this battle to get rich drive you till it becomes your whole life?"

"It's for Rusty to begin with," Bandine said angrily. "For him and Kit."

"Sometimes I think you are losing sight of that."

Bandine glanced sharply at him. There was a taut look to Chico's narrow face. Then he turned back to camp. Bandine watched him go, realizing Chico was right. It made him recall the other times he had tried to reach his kids, in the last years, and failed. He remembered forgetting Rusty's birthday that time, and promising him red-topped boots, and then being forced to break the promise to go out after the maverickers. He had lost something then in the boy—some bit of faith. And the time with the pony, letting Holichek goad him into a fight, losing his chance to fulfill his promise to both his kids. He had tried to make it up to them, buying a pair of gentled horses a week later. But it had not been the same; it had left the faint scars of disappointment and disillusionment in them. Maybe once wasn't so much, but when you added it all up, through the years, it gained weight.

How could a man want so much for his kids and yet be able to attain so little? It had been so simple in the beginning. He remembered that day, so shortly after Catherine's death, when he had made the bitter vow that his children would never know the poverty that had killed so many things dear to him.

Now, somehow, it seemed so obscured, so tainted by the other things—the bitter clashes remaining after the war, the struggle with the maverickers, the dirty politics in Austin—all pulling and pushing him till his whole life seemed to be taken up with fighting them. Adah had warned him long ago that he was letting this struggle to rise up in the world take him farther and farther from his kids. He hadn't seen it then. Now that he did see it, how could he stop? If he even slacked up, there were a dozen men like Big Bob who would pull him down. Everything he stood for was a threat to them. And it wasn't in him to give up the dream he had for his kids; he couldn't see them go back to the bitter poverty he had known as a boy.

A wave of anger swept him. Maybe he had got off the track, maybe he had been fighting so hard he had lost contact with Rusty and Kit. But it wasn't over yet. He wheeled and stalked back to camp, staring at his sleeping boy's face in the last of the firelight. Bandine could see how shaggy the brows were getting, just like his. Rusty was his son, and if he hadn't given him enough up to now, there was still time, damn it, there was still time.

XII

Chico Morales always rose before dawn, even before the cook was awake, dressing and walking out into the brush fringing camp for a smoke. From the pouch that every Mexican wore at his belt he took the bundle of *hojas*. Removing one of these corn-husk cigarette papers, he shook tobacco into it from a reed tube also carried in the pouch. Rolling the cigarette, he next took out the red cord of timber, the bit of flint, the steel *eslabón,* all wrapped in a piece of buckskin. With *eslabón* and flint, he struck a spark that lodged in the tinder. Blowing the spark into a flame, he lit his cigarette. Then he pinched out the flame in the tinder and returned all his primitive makings to the pouch. Finally he settled himself with a comfortable sigh and took his first deep drag on the cigarette.

It was a ritual belonging to the simplest of men, whose love of the land was one of the biggest things in his life. For he cherished this short time when he could have the brush to himself, drinking in its dawn scents, listening to the familiar rustlings of the small animals, watching the chaparral and mesquite take feathery shape in the growing pearly light.

This intense affinity with the land was the biggest reason Chico had refused Bandine's offer of partnership in the Double Bit. For even at that time he had seen the insidious influences of the struggle to rise weaning Bandine away from the land to which he, also, had belonged. And Chico's own love of the brush ran too deep and fierce to trade it for what was happening to Bandine. It frightened Chico, now, to see how Bandine's fight to get big was tearing his life apart. But he knew the bitter things driving the man, and felt helpless before them.

He saw more of it over breakfast that morning. Bandine took pains to explain to the boy exactly what their duties were during the day. Rusty showed polite interest but asked no questions when Bandine was through, and the conversation died. Chico saw the frustration in Bandine's eyes, felt pity for what was going on in him. Bandine was in painful search for words that would break the barriers between himself and his boy. But he had never been an articulate man and was helpless in his need for expression that would not come.

Perhaps it was the land itself that had left him that way. Few of the men who spent their lives in the loneliness of the brasada were at home with words. And having been nurtured by this land, Bandine bore its stamp. When it came to expressing the things nearest his heart, he was as inarticulate as the brush. For the thickets hid their heart from a stranger; a man had to know them a lifetime before learning their secrets.

The crew split up into twos and threes, each group taking a couple of neck oxen. As ramrod, Chico usually floated around among all the bunches, and he chose to ride with Bandine and Rusty for the first part of the morning. Though the maverickers and cattle operators had been working the thickets for seven years, since the war, they had not yet caught up with the incredible increase of unbranded cattle that had come during the four years of conflict. The thickets were still filled with mavericks anywhere from three to ten years old that had yet to be caught and branded. These were what Chico and Bandine flushed from the chaparral an hour out of camp.

It was a wild ride through the thickets, trying to catch those *cimarrónes*. Rusty was a good enough rider in the open, but as soon as they had to break brush, he ran into trouble. Chico saw him almost swept off by a mesquite branch, saw him duck to avoid a clawing arm of chaparral and almost lose his saddle. Then he was out of sight behind and Chico had all he could do to gather the beef. By the time he and Bandine got them into a mill and quieted them down, the boy had come up, sweating and panting, bleeding all over from brush scratches.

"You can't shut your eyes like that when you're popping the brush," Bandine told Rusty. "You got to keep them open all the time. How you going to see what's fixin' to knock you off if your eyes are shut?"

"I'll try to do better," the boy said. "I started to try and head them off from the east, but those other men were over there, and I figured they'd catch any that veered that way."

Bandine glanced sharply at Chico. "That can't be our bunch," he said. A sudden anger made his eyes glitter, and Chico knew what he was thinking. He asked Rusty: "Did they see you?"

"I don't think so. I just caught a glimpse of them through that real tall chaparral."

"You stay here, Rusty. No matter what happens, you stay here with the cattle."

Even as he said it, Bandine wheeled his horse and put it into a run down the trail Rusty had come in on. Chico glanced at the boy, then followed Bandine. They ran headlong for half a mile, then the chaparral loomed ahead of them, taller than a man on horseback. Through an open patch they saw the pear flat beyond and the two riders milling a cut of cattle.

It was maverickers, all right, and they evidently thought Bandine and Chico were some of their own crew, hazing a new cut of beef. They merely turned at the crash of brush, showing no surprise till Bandine burst into view. Then they wheeled their horses so hard one reared and almost pitched his rider. When they saw Bandine pulling his gun, they both spun around and spurred their horses off the flats. Bandine veered after them, shooting. But he didn't make a hit before they gained the brush.

"They're heading out Rusty's way!" he shouted. "Get on their flank and turn them, Chico!"

The Mexican was still in the chaparral and turned back, trying to quarter in on the two riders. But when he struck the trail, he saw that they had beaten him and were ahead. His horse was faster, and he had almost caught them when they reached the clearing where Rusty was holding the cattle. The sudden appearance of the two galloping riders stampeded the cattle and spooked Rusty's horse. Rusty lost control completely and a post-oak branch swept him from the saddle as the horse ran into the thickets.

Chico forgot the maverickers and veered over to where the boy had fallen. Swinging down, he saw Bandine appear from the trail. Bandine pulled his horse down hard, staring after the maverickers, who were just disappearing into the mesquite across the clearing. Chico saw the man's anger struggling against his concern for the boy, and knew Bandine wanted those maverickers in the worst way. Finally, however, he wheeled his lathered horse over to where Chico knelt above Rusty. The boy was still dazed, and they saw where a big coma thorn had caught him in the ankle joint. He cried out in pain when they pulled it free, and it left an ugly wound.

"Those things poison like a rattler," Bandine said. "He'll be swelled up like a calf with the bloat before we get him back to camp."

"We're nearer my place than camp," Chico said. "Why not take him there? Santero can cure anything like this."

They reached the Morales place near noon. The old man welcomed them warmly, showing great concern over the boy's wound. It was already beginning to swell, and the boy's face was flushed with fever. Santero put him to bed and made a poultice of prickly pear to draw the pus out. Then he insisted on soaking a dozen red peppers in a glass of mescal and giving it to the boy for his fever. But Bandine was not satisfied, and asked Chico to get the doctor from Spanish Crossing.

Bandine and Santero stayed awake most of that night with Rusty, while the boy tossed deliriously in the bunk. But toward dawn Rusty settled down, his breathing grew deep and regular. Sitting with his great frame bowed over the bed, Bandine felt Santero's hand on his shoulder.

"You see," the old man whispered. "The red peppers and Our Lady of Remedies, they would not let him die."

Bandine saw that the parchment-faced old man had brought one of his Mary statues to stand at the head of the bed, the turquoise blue of her robe shining dimly in the candlelight. A slow smile touched Bandine's mouth, and he grasped the old man's arm.

"I'd almost forgotten how it was."

Santero nodded somberly. "That is sometimes what I fear, Emery. I wish you would come back to the brush before it has lost you completely."

Bandine turned away, having no answer for that. He felt, too, that something was happening to his roots in this land. But it was all a part of the thing he had tried to fight out the night before, and he could still see no answer. He dozed till mid-morning and then awoke with Rusty. The boy felt well enough to down some of the beef and beans Santero fixed for them. After eating, the old man took the dishes out to clean them in the sand, leaving Bandine and Rusty alone. The boy was watching Bandine, and it seemed there was a deep boyish blame in his solemn eyes.

Well, Bandine thought, maybe the boy was right. Rusty hadn't wanted to come in the first place. Bandine had kicked him out of the sack at dawn and pushed him into some of the roughest riding in the world. If it hadn't been for his bull-headedness, this wouldn't have happened. He wanted to make it up, somehow, to apologize.

It struck him that he had never apologized to anybody in his life. It was a rare moment of insight. What a hell of a stiff-necked pride a man must have to go through life never apologizing to anybody, a pride that had probably betrayed him and cut him off from people more times than he would ever know. He couldn't let it betray him now. He felt it rising already, making him feel like a fool for being sentimental. He had to fight it to go to the boy and speak.

"Rusty," he said. "I'm sorry."

It sounded so inane, so inadequate. The boy looked up at him strangely, then turned his head to the wall, saying: "Never mind. I know you blame me for being such a greenhorn. If you hadn't had to stop for me, you could have gotten those maverickers."

"Is that what you've been thinking?" Bandine asked. "I thought you blamed me for making you get hurt."

"I wasn't even thinking about that."

Bandine knelt beside the bunk. "Those were only two maverickers out of a thousand, jigger. They don't mean a thing." He began to chuckle. "That's funny. I thought you blamed me and you thought I blamed you and we was really thinking about six other things. Don't you know a man ain't a brushpopper till he takes a hundred and seven spills? I got knocked off a dozen times my first day. Ain't you ever seen my lumps?"

Bandine pulled up his pants leg to show Rusty where the post oak had clouted him when he was seventeen. It still made a bump like an egg and the boy's eyes widened in owlish awe. One by one, then, they went over his lumps and scars, and Rusty had to know the story behind each one. They were still examining them and Bandine had got the boy to chuckling over the reminiscences when Chico appeared in the door. Bandine looked up to see how grimed with dust the man was, hollows of weariness sunken deeply into his bony young face.

"The doctor's coming as soon as he can," Chico said. "I

thought I'd better get right back. Waggoner come up from Austin special to let us know. The panic's spreading and the bottom may drop out of the beef market any day. Waggoner says the only way you can save yourself is to round up everything and dump it at the nearest market for whatever price you can get."

Bandine rose to his feet slowly, absently tucking his shirt back in over the scars on his hide. It took a moment for the shock of it to settle in him. Then he realized what would be necessary. Chico wasn't a driving enough man to handle a roundup of this type alone. Bandine would have to be out there himself, every minute of the time. It would be like those first roundups after the war, working their hearts out eighteen hours a day in a race against time. And there wasn't a minute to spare. At last he turned to Rusty.

"You understand, jigger?"

The boy had settled back into the bunk. All the humor had left his face. He stared solemnly and emptily up at his father.

"Yes," he said. "I understand."

Bandine stood there, wanting to say more, finding no words. Finally, helplessly, he turned to the door. Chico followed him, seeing the misery in his face, and put a hand on his shoulder.

"The boy will be all right here. When he is able to travel, Santero will take him home."

Bandine did not answer. It was not what had been in his mind. It was as if, all in a moment, he had found something precious and lost it again.

XIII

The panic of 1873 hit Dan Holichek as hard as anybody. It cut his cattle speculation out from under him and for a while he had to scratch hard to drum up enough penny-ante deals around town to keep him going. What really hurt was the fact that Bandine had managed to unload most of his beef before the bottom dropped out. He was one of the few big operators who had not been ruined in the panic, and was now only waiting for the market to rise.

By early in 1875 the nation was getting back on its feet. Two new railroads had reached Texas, providing nearer shipping points for the trail drivers. Bandine began building his herds again. Holichek renewed his alliance with the maverickers, and the old pattern began once more. But it was to be changed by a man named Glidden who had patented a new-fangled contraption called barbed wire in 1874.

The Spanish Crossing district was one of the first areas to use it, and by spring of 1876 the mavickers had a taste of what it meant. With fences beginning to criss-cross the prime thickets, and riders policing the fences, the brasada became a fortress to be stormed anew each time by the mavickers. If they cut a hole to get in, they could rarely use the same way back out, for it would have been discovered in the meantime. Once inside, they faced a maze of fences. If discovered, a run would sooner or later bring them up against a fence, with their pursuers giving them no time to cut a hole big enough for the cattle. Almost daily, mavickers were forced to give up their gather under these circumstances, and were lucky to escape with their hides. For the first time the big operators had a weapon that gave them the upper hand.

In their zeal they began fencing state land as well as their own. This often cut off the free graze and the watering places that for generations had been considered open to all. The small operators who had no alliance with the mavickers began to protest. But the big men paid no heed. Holichek saw a chance to align more of the brush men against Bandine and his faction, and, when he heard there was going to be a meeting of the smaller operators at Santero Morales's, he rode out to attend.

He took the Laredo road and was passing Bandine's house,

gleaming like a marble castle on its hill overlooking the river, when he saw Rusty riding toward him from the bottoms. Holichek had not seen the boy lately, and was surprised at how he had sprouted. He was almost as tall as Holichek, his hair growing in shaggy, rust-red hanks down the back of his neck. The man saluted him, grinning, and Rusty checked his horse, studying Holichek gravely.

Holichek sensed what was on his mind and chuckled huskily. "I know you've seen your dad and me have our differences in the past. But he's always misreading me. I'm not a troublesome man at heart. Why don't we put up the truce flag and have a talk?"

Without smiling, Rusty managed to convey a sheepish humor. He dismounted with the intensely self-conscious awkwardness of the adolescent. He started to shove his hands in his pockets and then, as if not quite knowing what to do with them, changed his mind and hooked bony thumbs in the belt of his jeans. As young and coltish as he seemed, there was something disturbingly mature in the sober expression on his face.

"You're growin' like a weed," Holichek said. "When you going to take over that cattle business from your dad?"

Holichek saw his infallible geniality begin to get under the boy's skin. Rusty would obviously take longer than most men to thaw out, but a hesitant lowering of his reserve was noticeable. He seemed to consider the question carefully, then said: "I think I'd rather be a lawyer, sir."

"Call me Dan," Holichek said. He took out a cigar, paring at it with his penknife. "A lawyer, is it? That's not a bad line." He saw faint surprise cross the boy's freckled face and glanced at him from beneath bushy black brows. "What's the matter? Nobody else taking it seriously?"

The boy shook his head slowly. "You know what Dad would say. Nothing but the cattle business. He almost had a fit when I first told him I wanted to be a lawyer. Jerry Waggoner listened to me. But he was just humoring me. I could tell. I guess they think I'm too young to know what I want to do."

"In some ways, you're probably much older than they realize," Holichek said. Then, on a sudden, wry whim, he offered the cigar to Rusty. Holichek knew it was something that had a universal intrigue for boys of that age. He remembered the delicious sense of sin that had come to him when he stole a smoke on a corn-shuck cigarette behind the barn, as a youth. As advanced as Rusty was, in some ways, there was still enough boyishness in him to react. Holichek saw his eyes glow for a moment, then he soberly shook his head. "Go ahead," Holichek urged. "If you're going to be a lawyer, you got to smoke cigars. Why do you think I took it up?"

Rusty's lips parted. "You?"

"Sure. I studied for the law. But I never could stick to one thing long. All those books to read. I had too many other irons in the fire, I guess. I still got some books. There's one that might not be over your head. Pomeroy's *Equity Jurisprudence*. Don't let the title scare you. There's some chapters you could understand."

More of the reserve left Rusty; awe made him seem younger. "Gee . . . Dan. . . ."

"Sure." Holichek clapped him on the back. "Next time you're in town, look me up at O'Hara's. We'll go through the books together. Now." He jabbed the smoke at Rusty. "How about that seegar?"

Hesitantly Rusty took it, gripping the smoke tentatively between his teeth. Holichek lighted it for him, then got one for himself. They stood a moment, puffing conscientiously, wreathed in the comradeship of fragrant smoke.

"Gee, Dan. . . ." Rusty coughed a little. "I didn't think you were like this. The names Dad has called you, in that house. . . ."

Holichek stamped his foot, chuckling heartily. "I guess I have aggravated him in the past. You got to understand why, Rusty. Your pa's a big operator now, and I'm still a little one. But he was a little operator, too, once. He forgets that at one time he was fighting for the same things all the little operators are fighting for now. Just a chance for survival, a chance to live their life out on a few acres, run a few cattle, know a little contentment."

Rusty removed the cigar, looking a little pale. "Dad says they're at his throat. If he gave an inch, they'd pull him down."

Holichek shook his head sadly. "Of course you don't get the true picture from your pa. And if you're going to be a lawyer, Rusty, you better start learning the truth of these matters." He glanced shrewdly at the boy, something growing in his mind. "I'm going to a meeting of the little operators at Santero's right now. This fence business is threatening their very existence. Why not come along? You'll get a different viewpoint for a change."

A momentary eagerness flooded the boy's face, then he looked at the ground, shook his head. "They wouldn't want me."

"Why not? Santero practically raised you. They know you ain't as bull-headed as your dad."

The boy started to speak, but broke into a fit of coughing.

With an affectionate laugh, Holichek slapped the cigar from his hand. "I guess that's enough the first time. You can't ride if you're sick. Come with me, now. It's about time you learned a few things."

Rusty had trouble mounting his horse, and swayed a little when he reached the saddle. Holichek tightened his girth and swung up. Rusty started out in the lead, and Holichek followed, watching his bony young shoulders thoughtfully. It would be nice to have a boy like that, he thought.

He sensed a reaching out in Rusty, like some plant seeking the sun, and was convinced that he had answered some of the need in these few minutes. He had often seen the boy with his father in town. Something in their manner, along with Holichek's own knowledge of Bandine, had convinced him that some kind of gap lay between father and son. It gave him a sense of triumph to feel that he could reach the youth where Bandine could not. But more than that, it struck at deeper yearnings in him that were dormant most of the time. It made him realize how devoid of any relationships like this his life was. It made him think, somehow, of his age. Thirty-seven, and not married yet. How swiftly the years passed.

Then he shook off the mood. What the hell was the matter with him? There had been more in his mind than just entertaining a lonely boy for an hour. It was returning now, the thought that had reached him when he invited Rusty to join him at Santero's. It was still vague, because he couldn't yet see how it could be used. Yet it was there. Just how lonely was the boy, and how far could he be cultivated? Bandine's love of his kids was probably the most powerful thing in his life. What a weapon it would be, if it could be turned against him.

Claire heard a lot about the fence trouble that spring, for her father had a fence-cutting complaint before him almost daily. But it did not touch her personally till that last Sunday in June. She had spent most of the morning supervising the Sunday dinner, but finally she left Pearl and the savory odors of the kitchen to seek out her father. As she moved through the cool chasm of the center hall, she found herself taking a quiet pride in what she had managed to accomplish with the house these last years. The burned east wing had been entirely rebuilt, the broken window glass was replaced, tapestry carpets took the place of the tattered Aubussons that had revealed their poverty so clearly the day Bandine had come to make the Wolf Sink deal. There was even a new console and big pier mirror in the entrance hall,

its frame gilded with matte that glimmered dully in the half
light. She halted momentarily before it, touching her enamel-
black braids, rearranging the frothy collar of her cool dimity
dress. Then she moved into the library.

Her father was seated at a table by the open French windows,
his books and briefs scattered across its marble top. His face
was drawn and tired, and he was leaning on one elbow, pinching the bridge of his nose. His hair was all gray now, and she
was struck with how much he had aged in the last years. The
loss of Webb had been the biggest factor, she knew. They hardly
heard from the boy any longer. The last time was a year ago,
when he had written from some mining camp in Colorado.

Claire walked over and blew out the lamp, wrinkling her
nose. "We'll have to get some fresh camphene. That's beginning
to smell like turpentine again."

"I wasn't through," he protested mildly.

"Yes, you were. Up till three o'clock last night, and now all
this morning. If you must study the rest of these briefs, I'll read
them to you after you've taken a nap."

He chuckled indulgently. "I don't know what I'd do without
you. Run the most efficient household in the world, and that on
a pittance." He shook his head. "I hate to see you scrimping
and saving and cutting so many corners."

"Is that why you're going to run for state senator?"

He rose, tucking thumbs into his suspenders, and walked
thoughtfully across the room. "It would mean more money, but
that isn't the prime consideration. This fight between the big
operators and the maverickers is going to tear the country apart
unless it's settled. I want to do something, but I feel so
inadequate, on the bench. All I can do is hand down decisions
or charge the jury, and the fighting goes right on. It's been so
completely partisan up to now, in Austin. I'm sure that an
arbitrator with the respect of both sides could bring them

together and settle it."

"But why must you throw in with Big Bob?"

"Obviously I can't run on the Democratic ticket, my dear, and I can't make it alone. . . ."

"But Bob doesn't rightly belong to any party, Dad. He and his bunch are the dirtiest politicians in Austin, just affiliating themselves with whoever they think can do them the most good. They were hand in glove with Davis. . . ."

"Which was no crime," Nadell said. "Davis may have been misguided, but I'm convinced he was utterly sincere. Bob has fought for a lot of fine things. It's on record that he's been pushing this new school bond for years. . . ."

"Which makes a marvelously pious smoke screen for the dirty deals he pulls under the table."

"You forget how much time I spent in Austin, Claire. Bob has enemies, any man in politics has. But I never saw any proof to back up these accusations against him. He's promised me the support on every plank I specified. . . ."

"And the minute you're elected they'll start forcing you to compromise. They don't want any maverick arbitration. This clash between the big operators and the little ones is the only thing that has kept Bob's bunch in business. All they want is your good name to suck some more fools in behind their machine. . . ."

"Now, now, Claire." He walked to her, putting a hand on her shoulder. "I think your feelings for Bandine are swaying you. He hates both the Holicheks and you're letting it color your own thinking."

Her eyes widened a little in surprise. She had told Webb how she felt about Bandine, never her father.

Nadell chuckled indulgently. "You may think I'm blind to some things, but I've known you were in love with Bandine for a long time. It shows, when he's around."

"And you aren't angry?"

He frowned thoughtfully. "At first, I suppose I was. But perhaps the years have mellowed me. Bandine doesn't seem so much the villain any more. He's caught up in this just like the rest of us. The whole thing is another inevitable cycle, like the war, and most of us are pawns, little and big, pushed this way and that. . . ." He broke off to grin wryly. "But that sounds sententious, doesn't it? And we were talking about you. You usually get what you go after, but I must say you have a peculiar way of going after Bandine."

She looked down at her hands, locked together. "I have to wait for something."

"His wife?"

She nodded faintly. "Catherine is still with Bandine. It wouldn't matter if all these other issues no longer stood between us. She'd still be there. And I can't do anything about that."

He sighed. "I suppose you're right. Time alone will have to heal it. I never had the desire to marry again, after your mother's death. But not a man like Bandine. He's too vital, too earthy. No matter how much he loved Catherine, I can't see him going without a woman for the rest of his life."

She looked up at him again, feeling he had struck a truth. "How can you see these things so clearly, in Bandine, and yet be so blind to what goes on in Holichek?"

He frowned, then turned from her, walking to the window, staring out. "I still think you're maligning Holichek. But perhaps I'm wrong. It has always been the dark side of men, their violence, their evil that has left me feeling so baffled and impotent. Perhaps some men were meant to understand only the gentle side. Perhaps that's why I see these things in Bandine."

She was silent for a moment, feeling closer to her father in that moment than she had been in a long time. Before she could speak again, Pearl's boy came hesitantly to the door. He said there were some men outside who wished to see the judge. Nadell told Leander to let them in and turned to get his coat. He had it on when the trio of men appeared, holding their hats in their hands, spurs clattering on the floor. It was Santero Morales and the half-breed Revere and a white man Claire did not know.

"There is a dozen more of us outside," Santero told Nadell. "We ask you to come with us, Judge. We are go to Bandine, in a last effort to end this fence trouble before it ruins us completely."

XIV

That day had been an unfortunate choice, for Santero and the others. Kit was leaving for Kansas City. She was fourteen now, and already most of the other daughters of the bigger cattlemen had been sent to finishing schools in the East. Last year Cathy Innes had started at Miss Primm's in Kansas City, and Kit had been pleading to join her ever since. Bandine had never been able to deny his daughter anything, and he had finally yielded to social as well as personal pressure. It was in reality one of the saddest moments of his life.

For a long time he had felt much closer to Kit than to Rusty. Sometimes it seemed that she was really all he had left. With her vivid, youthful beauty and her bubbling nature, she was beloved by everyone. His enforced absences did not seem to form the gap between them, the way they did with Rusty. She met him with as much gaiety and affection as if he had not been gone an hour. It was his pride and joy to take her driving into town, or to one of the other big houses along the river. Sometimes he thought her endless prattle about gowns and boys and cotillions was rather empty, but it gave him a sense of ease with her that he never knew with Rusty. Although she seemed to do most of the talking when they were together, he could still amuse her with a wry comment, and even the Grandpa Willoughby stories sent her into gales of laughter, if he caught her in the right mood.

He felt morose as an old bull sulking out in the thickets, as he sat alone in the library, listening to the bustle of preparations for departure fill the house. He had felt left out of it from the moment he had agreed that she could go. She had become forever closeted with Adah, in an endless discussion of what to wear and what to do, and then there had been the packing, in which he could be no help at all.

Kit darted past the door, fresh and prim in a new calico dress, and then stopped and came back to peek around the edge. "You'd better get dressed. Almost time to go."

"Kit," he said, "come here a minute."

She came in, holding a handful of hair ribbons, a puzzled look on her face. He beckoned her to come on until she stood beside the worn leather armchair. He gazed up at her, thinking how much she looked like Catherine. Then he reached up to twine his fingers in her corn-yellow hair, the way he had done so often before. With a little giggle, she pushed his hand away.

"You'll muss it."

He dropped his hand back to the chair arm, sighing heavily. Why was he always so inadequate with words? Even with her, now. Wanting to express the loss this meant to him, unable to find the right words.

"Kit."

"Yes, Dad."

"You'll miss me?"

"Of course I will, old silly." She leaned down to peck him on the forehead, then turned to go. He caught her hand, holding her back a moment longer.

"You'll come back next summer, you promise."

"I will, I will. Where else would I go? Now I've got to rush, or we'll be late for the stage."

He let her go reluctantly, watched her hurry through the door. He felt a stab of restlessness and rose to follow her, turning toward the front, his great cartwheel spurs clattering destructively across the mottled red Sienna marble.

"Emery," Adah called, rushing through the parlor, "how often I got to ask you to take them things off in the house?"

He barely heard her. He had gained the verandah and started to go down the steps when he saw the riders turning off the river road and coming up through the gate. There must have been a dozen of them, with a buckboard in the lead. He realized with a start that Claire and her father were in the rig.

Some of the Double Bit crew drifted out of the bunkhouse to watch the cavalcade pass, and then began to follow them up to the big house. Bandine saw that Santero was among the riders, and Revere and Pancho and the Graves brothers and half a dozen other men he had run with in the brush long ago. They halted their animals before the verandah with a creaking of leather, and the sour sweat smell of man and beast was carried to him. The sober tension in their faces kept him from the usual invitation to light and set a while. Santero took out his bandanna, wiping the briny sweat from the myriad grooves of his face.

"I guess you know why we are here," the old man said in his whispery voice. "It is about the fences. They ask me to talk, for I know you best. We cannot take it any more. The last fence you put up across Mexican Thickets cuts off all the southern operators from Blue Sink."

"Then use the river."

"You know I can't drive that far every time I need water," Revere said angrily.

"The mavericks were cleaning out Mexican Thickets," Bandine said. "If I pull the fence down to let you through, they'd be right back at it."

Nadell took off his flat-topped hat, running a finger around the soggy sweatband. "They asked me along as sort of an arbitrator, Bandine. In the early days of mavericking, my sympathies lay mostly with the little men. But this fence cutting has become so flagrant that only a blind man could continue to hold you big operators completely to blame for all the trouble. At the same time, you and Innes and the others control so much of the brush that, if you continue to fence the way you are, you'll cut off access to all the little man's water. If you could only meet them halfway on this thing. . . ."

"I'll meet them halfway. You get me a law that will stop mavericking and I'll pull all my fences down."

Nadell's nostrils pinched in, and a baffled anger rose into his face. Before he could speak again, Santero said: "You are forcing the decent operators to join the maverickers and the fence cutters, Emery. I persuaded these men to come and try to talk it out. But there are hundreds of others in the brush waiting to hear how it comes out."

Bandine heard a soft stir behind him and it made him think of Kit, waiting to go. "You picked a bad day for this," he said irritably. "My girl's leaving for Kansas City and I haven't got any more time to talk. It wouldn't do no good anyway. You know I can't do what you ask, Santero."

A creaking of leather ran through the group as the riders began to stir. Revere was first to move, wheeling his horse around, saying angrily: "I told you it wouldn't do no good."

Nadell stood up in the buckboard, raising a hand. "Now, men, wait a minute. . . ."

"Save your breath, Nadell," Billy Graves said thinly. "We're through talking."

As the dust rose thickly about the wheeling horses, Santero settled into his cactus-tree saddle. His face was like parchment and the bird-like sharpness had gone from his eyes, leaving them dull and lifeless. Bandine felt a sudden relenting, and went down the steps to catch the horse's bit before Santero could turn away.

"This can't be for you, old one," he said in a soft voice. "You know whatever I have is yours. Run your cattle in my thickets. Use my water."

Santero's skinny body straightened like a ramrod. An intense pride gave his face a hawk-like profile. "I am of the brush, Emery. My life is there and my people are there. I cannot turn on them like that. I cannot make myself an outcast."

The seams of his face were engraved so deeply by the pride and the hurt that they looked like wounds, as he pulled his horse around till the bit slipped from Bandine's hand. Bandine stood helplessly, watching the old man go. Finally he saw Claire stir in the buckboard. Her father tried to restrain her with a hand on her arm, but she pulled free and climbed down and walked over to Bandine. She touched his arm gently. He spoke in a bitter voice, still watching Santero.

"Can't they see what a bind I'm in? The maverickers were ruining me before I started fencing. If I let my fences down now, I might as well quit."

"And if you don't let them down, you'll lose every friend you have in the brush."

The compassion of her voice made him look at her for the first time. "You would have been with them a few years ago," he said.

"And I would have been making a mistake," she said. "You don't need argument, Emery. You need help. Is there anything at all I can do?"

Her face was uplifted to him, her underlip full and soft, her gray eyes smoky. He realized it was the same way she had looked that day just before the kiss in the courthouse, so long ago. It removed the bitterness of this moment and took him back to that kiss.

He couldn't remember how often he had thought about it, afterward. Up to that time it had never occurred to Bandine that another woman could take Catherine's place. He had not been blind to Claire's beauty. But he had thought of it merely in its physical terms, had thought that his love of Catherine was too great to get over in one lifetime.

With that kiss, his whole feeling had undergone a change. It had made him realize how long he had been without a woman, had made the great house on the river seem suddenly useless and unbearably empty, an emptiness that even Kit and his love for his kids could not quite fill. There had been vague feeling of betraying Catherine. But in his heart he knew that was not logical, knew that Catherine would not have blamed him. He had become suddenly conscious of other men who had married again, after a wife's death, and who seemed completely happy. The passing years had dimmed the vision of Catherine that he carried with him, and had increased his doubt and his wonder. But if the memory of Catherine was less poignant than before, it still remained. It would take more than a kiss and the passage of a few years to remove it.

He wondered if Claire saw that in him, as she stood looking up into his face. He wondered if it was what held her back, kept her from expressing the thing that gave her face that strange, poignant expression. He heard the stir in the doorway again and knew that time had run out.

"Thank you, ma'am," he said. "But I guess there's nothing you can do about this."

"I'm sorry for you, Emery. I'm truly sorry."

She looked into his eyes a moment longer, then turned back to the buckboard. He watched her go, filled with a deep frustration. Then, with a curse, he wheeled to the steps. He saw that

Rusty stood on the verandah, with Kit and Adah in the door, and the rest of the household gathered behind them in the entrance hall. Kit came to meet him as he approached the door.

"Dad," she said, "I wish I didn't have to go now."

"I'm sorry you had to see that," he said, "but we haven't got time to talk if you want to catch that stage."

She smiled reassuringly and squeezed his hand, then turned to go back in. He looked at Rusty, tried to grin. "Put your coat on, jigger, and go down and get the wagon for us."

Rusty did not move. That intense soberness of his bony young face made it look years older, and his eyes were fixed darkly on Bandine. "You aren't going to go through with it," he said. "You aren't going to leave those fences up."

"You, too?" Bandine said sharply. Anger tightened the flesh across his cheek bones till they had a sharp, raw shape. "How can you talk that way? You know better than anybody what that mavericking was doing to me before we got the fences."

"And I know what it's doing to the brushpoppers now. I was out to Santero's, Dad. His cattle are dying off without water. You can't do that to your old friends. Revere helped you get your start. Santero was like a father to you."

"Rusty, don't you think I know all that?"

The boy's eyes ceased to focus on Bandine and his face grew stiff and set. It seemed to withdraw him completely. "Mister Dalhart says you've built a cattle empire. All I can see is you've got a choice now, between your friends and your empire. . . ."

"Not my empire, jigger. *Your* empire. All I did was for you and Kit. You know that. If I quit now, you'll lose it all. We'll be back to linsey-woolsey on our backs and starving all winter if the mesquite bean crop goes rotten. Don't you remember how hard it was?"

The boy straightened his knobby shoulders. "If that's the reason you're doing it, you can stop right now. I don't want it on these terms. Kit wouldn't, either."

"Now you're talking like a fool. You're too young to under-stand this. Go get your coat."

A sullen stubbornness settled into the boy's face, giving his lower lip that full, square shape Bandine knew so well. He balled his bony fists and jammed them into his pockets. "I don't want to go to town with you."

"Damn you . . . !" In a violent impulse over which he had no control, Bandine caught the boy by the shirt with one hand and drew the other back to slap him. He checked himself, then, re-alizing how far his rage had taken him. Rusty was rigid in his grasp, face white and stiff.

"Go ahead," he said. "Like I was a kid or something."

Bandine settled back, releasing the boy, dropping his hand. There was an ashen taste in his mouth. He looked into his son's face and it was like looking into the face of a stranger. He turned and walked into the library, closing the door behind him, stand-ing against it, trying to collect the pieces of the day that had been shattered about him. Finally he became aware of Mr. Dal-hart, standing by the open French windows.

"I didn't mean to eavesdrop," the man said. "But I couldn't help overhear. You're wrong about Rusty, Mister Bandine. He isn't too young to understand. You'll lose him completely if you don't quit treating him like a child."

Bandine knew deep resentment of the man in that moment, feeling that his anger and defeat and helplessness were an intensely private thing to him, which no man had the right to see or pry into. The day had been too much for him and he was filled with the boiling need to strike back at something.

"I think you're one of the reasons I'm losing him, Dalhart. He's been spending more time with you than he has with me for years, in here with those books and those fool notions you put in his head. . . ."

"He had to turn to someone, Mister Bandine, with you gone so much."

"Well, he won't any more. It's time he quit wasting his time in the parlor and came out to learn the cattle business. I think your use is over here. Kit's gone now, and Rusty won't be needing you any more."

Dalhart's narrow, patrician head bowed, and he spoke in a soft voice. "I knew it would come, sooner or later. A boy can't have two fathers." He looked up quickly, shyly. "But be careful, Mister Bandine. Don't try to force him into anything. You'll lose him irrevocably if you do."

"I don't need any advice on how to raise my boy. You can go now."

After Dalhart had left, Bandine stalked morosely around the room. He had long felt that Dalhart was one of the things standing between him and Rusty and had long meant to get rid of him. But now he found no satisfaction in it. He felt like a fool. He felt worse than ever. In a sudden fit of frustrated rage he swept a decanter of wine off the table and flung it savagely through the French windows. It broke the glass with a great crash and then smashed all over the verandah and the wine spread across the granite in a dark stain.

XV

During the last of that year the fence-cutting war spread like a plague. As more and more fencing went up, it became increasingly difficult to patrol it all. With the legitimate shoe-string operators in with the maverickers now, the ranks of the fence cutters was doubled. There were countless clashes in the thickets, but they achieved little. With no charge but trespass or property damage to bring against the cutters, the sheriff was helpless. When it did come to a trial, there was so much sympathy with the little men that a jury could not be found that would convict one of them.

The legislature recessed during the summer and Waggoner was in Spanish Crossing for a few brief weeks. He told Bandine that it was the same situation mavericking had put them in— their only hope lay in a bill making fence cutting a felony. But they needed a precedent, some definite proof that the cutting was an organized attempt to pull down the big ranchers. Thus the ranchers agreed to make a concerted drive against the fence cutters, with Sheriff Geddings along to make it official, catching enough of them red-handed to make an example of them.

They did not know where the fence cutters meant to strike next. They did know that whenever a new fence was erected it immediately became a target. Bandine had just leased a strip of state land along the Frío and put up his fences, and it was one of the spots they picked. After Bandine got home, he invited Chico up to the house for a drink. It was a moment he had long dreaded, but he knew it had to be met. Sensing the same thing on Chico's mind, he was careful to tell the Mexican only the general plan. The big operators had no hope of keeping that from being known anyway, with so many in their crews sympathetic to the little men. Their only hope lay in keeping secret the spot where they would strike. As Bandine talked, he saw the misery fill Chico's face, saw him put his drink down untasted.

"I suppose we both knew this moment would come sooner or later, Emery," Chico said. "I can no longer be your foreman. I cannot go out and fight my own father."

Bandine put his hand on his friend's shoulder. "I can tell you this much, Chico. We're not going to hit any place near Santero's pastures."

"What is the difference? He is against you now. Sooner or later you will meet him. I cannot go on like that, Emery."

Bandine turned savagely away from him, striking his fist into his palm. "I've asked myself a thousand times, Chico. Why does it have to be this way?"

"You could end it, Emery. . . ."

"And lose everything?" Bandine wheeled back. "How many times have we gone over that, Chico? It's even worse than it was with just the maverickers. I'm fighting for my life, Chico."

"And so are we, Emery."

They stood silently, staring at each other in complete and miserable helplessness. Then Chico turned and went out. Bandine stood at the window, watching the man saddle up in the corral, watching him say his good byes, watching him ride out into the brush. It left a deep and aching hurt in Bandine, and he knew it would be there a long time.

Bandine made George Remington his ramrod the next day and gave him his orders. The crew was to be sent out to the Frío fence in twos and threes, as any movement of a big body of men through the thickets would not escape the notice of the fence cutters. The crews of the other big ranchers would gather that way, as well as a posse. Bandine went out the next day and found most of them camped along the river. Sheriff Geddings came in near evening, a quiet, graying man about forty with a slow-moving, thick-bodied competence about him. They broke up into groups and scattered along the fence, half a mile apart. And then the wait began.

Nothing happened that night or the next. Riders came in with news of other fences being cut. The men began to grow restless. Innes got fed up and wanted to leave. A couple of Geddings's posse deserted. Bandine knew he couldn't hold them together much longer.

The moon came early the third night, rising over the undulant horizon of brush like a great yellow caravel swinging into view on a dark sea. The shadows beneath the thickets then became inky pools, and the silhouetted chaparral etched skeleton patterns against the luminous sky. Bandine was on watch with George Remington while the rest stayed in camp down by the river. Remington was a big, work-roughened man with great knob-knuckled hands that kept lifting to his shirt pocket.

"You want a smoke that bad, go on back to camp," Bandine said. "They'll see your light out here."

"Nobody to see it," Remington said indifferently. "Chico told his pappy for sure."

"He didn't have nothing to tell him," Bandine said. "The whole brush probably knows what we're planning by now. But they don't know where we are and they ain't going to stop cutting fences just for that. . . ."

He broke off as he saw Remington's bearded jaw lift. He heard it himself, then, the ping of a cut wire. Bandine nodded at Remington and the man snaked away to warn the others. Then Bandine picked up his .45-70 and crawled toward the pinging. He finally reached a mesquite tree from which he could see the shadowy shape at the fence. The man had cut his hole and was peeling the wires back. He went back for his horse then and rode through and headed northward along the gleaming track of wires. That meant he was scouting for a fence rider. After a long while he came back and rode down the other way. While he was gone in that direction, the brush began to rustle, and Remington and the others joined Bandine. Finally the horseman came back and rode out through the hole. They knew he was going to get the cattle, now, and settled down for the last wait.

After a short while there was a loud popping of brush, and the rider again appeared, at the point of a small herd. They were wild and jumpy steers, long horns clattering against each other, eyes rolling spookily. There were two men on swing and another pair bringing up the drag. The sour and acrid reek of sweat and dust swept to Bandine as the leaders passed where he was hiding. With the crash of brush to cover his voice, Bandine spoke to Remington.

"I'll take a man and keep up with those leaders. You stay here till the drag is past. We want all of 'em."

He began to crawl through the thickets, nodding at a man named Karnes, and the man followed him. They got past the swing riders without being seen. But as they drew abreast of the point man, Karnes rose too high in the brush. The rider saw it and shouted: "Henry, there's somebody else out here!"

Bandine jumped into the open with his rifle, shouting: "Pull up and raise your hands over your heads! It's pointblank and we're all around you."

The leader checked his horse in a startled way, and started to lift his hands. But the man on swing wheeled his animal around and dragged his gun out to shoot. The bullet made a clatter through the brush by Bandine's head. He swung his rifle, squeezing the trigger in sheer reflex. He heard the man shout and saw him clutch his leg, and then pitch out of the saddle.

The shots had spooked the cattle and they started running. The lead rider was on Bandine's side. His horse began to fiddle but did not run. He was silhouetted above the bobbing ridgepole backs of the cattle, and knew it. He kept his hands up, shouting hoarsely: "Don't shoot, I ain't done nothing!"

There was more firing from the rear of the herd. Bandine saw that the drag riders had tried to get back through the hole, but the fire of the Double Bit men had turned them down the fence. He knew that would take them into Sheriff Geddings. If the sheriff turned them back, they would probably veer off toward the river to keep from coming back into Bandine's crew.

"Karnes," Bandine called, "keep this one covered and get him down off his animal!" He saw Karnes running up to get the lead rider, and then he wheeled and began to run. The cattle were past, and he took a direction that would bisect the line those two drag riders would logically take when Geddings turned them back.

Even as he ran, he heard the shots begin from down the line. After the wild crashing of the cattle died, he heard more brush popping. It was getting louder, and coming back toward him in the direction he had counted on. He kept running to get across in front of them.

The brush clawed at his hat, his rawhide jacket, his churning legs, as he ran headlong for high land. He reached the toe of the ridge and ran up its spine till he was above the brush. Then he could see them coming, sharply etched by the moonlight, a pair of hard-pressed riders, weaving and ducking through patches of mesquite. As they reached the base of the ridge, he bawled at them: "Pull up! We've got you on both sides!"

They veered off at the sound of his voice, paralleling the ridge, and one began to shoot. Bandine ran down the slope toward them, answering the fire. His second shot struck one of the horses and it reared with a squeal, pitching the rider. The man hit hard and rolled and then came to a stop. At the same time the other rider saw that Bandine would cross in front of him, and pulled his horse up, wheeling indecisively. He had a gun out but made no move to fire, and Bandine called: "Stop there! I don't want to shoot you."

Whoever was in pursuit was making a great crash, coming through the brush from behind the rider. The man wheeled back. Bandine was still running toward him, and recognized him for the first time. He lowered his rifle and ran on up to the horse, catching the bridle.

"Santero, how did you get mixed up in this?"

Santero sagged heavily into the saddle, staring down at Bandine with a slack and defeated face. "My cattle had to have water, Emery, and your fence riders in Mexican Thicket cut me off from Blue Sink. I didn't know this was your fence."

"You fool, I leased this land six months ago," Bandine said. He flung the reins from him, stepping back. The crash of pursuit through the brush was almost upon them. "Get out, Santero. You can still do it. Nobody knows what happened here."

Santero glanced at the man who had been pitched from his horse, lying unconscious on the ground. Then that intense pride drew the old Mexican up. "You are still asking me to desert my friends and become your man. You can own all the land in the brush, but you cannot own a man's soul. I have made my choice. I will abide by it."

"Santero, please don't do it this way. . . ."

But the old man refused to move, in the few precious seconds he could have used to escape, and then Hammond Innes and half a dozen riders came clattering out of the brush and flooded around them. A man Bandine recognized as one of Geddings's deputies rode broadside into Santero, peering at his face.

"Which one of you shot Sheriff Geddings?"

"What does it matter?" Innes said bitterly. "Both these men were shooting. It don't look like Geddings will last back to town. If he dies, they'll both hang."

XVI

On June 20, 1877, Webb Nadell returned to Spanish Crossing. Clattering across the stone bridge in the scarred Concord, he saw how little the town had changed. The same line of adobe buildings ran four blocks down Cabildo, their blank walls as yellow as buckskin in the simmering heat. A new frame hotel had been put up beyond the Martinez house, but the cruel weather of the land had already peeled most of its paint off and warped its siding. The hostler ran out the fresh team with a rattle of harness, the sweat dripping off his chin and staining his shirt beneath the arms.

Webb stepped reluctantly into the powdery dust before the stage station, squinting his eyes against the blazing sun. He had changed more than the town. He had gained a man's weight, and it gave him an elegant figure in his tailored steel-pen coat. His face seemed even more wedge-shaped than ever, with the fine waxen pallor that came to a man when he spent his life indoors. He knew he would have to rent a horse to ride home on, and began to walk toward the livery. Sweating men stood listlessly in the shade of the Hastings House overhang, wiping their flushed necks with soggy bandannas, spitting idly at the wheel ruts scarring Cabildo. Webb let his eyes run carefully over them before he passed. He was past the age of deluding himself. He knew the face he sought.

And when he was opposite O'Hara's, he found it. The inevitable crowd of idlers loitered on the cracker barrels before the *cantina*. The center of the group was a broadly framed man in a black coat and a flat-topped hat, making emphatic gestures with his cigar as he talked. Someone caught sight of Webb and said something and the man with the cigar turned, and Webb was looking across the street into the black and dancing eyes of Dan Holichek.

The man's heavy brows raised in surprise, then he dipped his head at Webb and started across the street, followed by most of the group.

Webb waited in a sort of gray level between apprehension and indifference. Holichek halted at the curb, planting his boots widely and tilting his head back to look up at Webb. He was grinning, and he spoke with his strong teeth clenched around his cigar.

"Ten years, Webb. I hope I didn't keep you away that long."

A rough chuckle ran through the crowd, and Webb said: "No, not that long."

"What brings you back?"

"I guess I got homesick," said Webb. There was a stiff pause and he saw the waiting speculation in the men's faces and the sparring suddenly disgusted him. "Shall I keep out of the back alleys?" he asked sardonically.

Holichek chuckled ruefully, running a thumb through his black spade beard. "I will admit I was fit to kill you that night. But I'm not one to hold a grudge ten years."

Webb smiled with little humor. He still sensed some sly malice behind Holichek's bland smile, but there was no point in discussing it further.

"What's the latest word around O'Hara's, then?" he asked. "Last time I read the *Galveston News,* Morales's trial was the big thing. I never did understand how they could convict him, if Sheriff Geddings wasn't even killed."

"They never even proved who shot the sheriff," Holichek said disgustedly. "Both this Ketland and Santero were in on it, and so many guns going off nobody could tell where the bullet came from."

"I understand even Bandine tried his best to get Santero off."

Holichek nodded. "Geddings was crippled up by the bullet, you know, and it swung public sympathy against the fence cutters. The big operators figured they could use the case as an example to push the bill through making fence cutting a felony. They overrode Bandine and whipped up the feeling till Ketland and Santero didn't have a chance."

"That's too bad," Webb said. "Santero was as pure as a child."

"We'll get him off. We've got an appeal pending right now. We've got proof that the big operators are trying to railroad this through without regard to the facts of the case."

They stood silently a moment, with Holichek's hat brim hiding his face as he stared at the ground. Then he looked up at Webb again. "Guess you'll be seeing your folks, first. They're in town, you know. Probably at the inn now."

"I'll see you later, then."

"You do that." Holichek sucked on his cigar, smiling secretively at its glowing tip, and then exhaled a stream of fragrant smoke. "You do that, Webb."

Webb turned up the street with the feeling of some unresolved malice behind him. He heard a rough gust of laughter rise from the men, and felt a faint flush stain his cheeks. But he kept himself from turning to look and walked on to the inn. Just before he stepped under the first arcade he saw his father and Claire come from the door. The old man had aged noticeably. His hair was turning white, and the vertical grooves between his brows had deepened, giving him the look of a perpetual frown. But it was Claire who struck Webb most.

Twenty-nine, now, in the full bloom of her beauty, she was bigger than he remembered, a statuesque bigness that filled out her dress of blue satin with deep and ripened curves. Her eyes widened with surprise when she saw Webb, then she and the major were both coming swiftly to him. There was that first moment, without reserve, in which Claire took him in her arms and the major pounded him on the back, and they were all talking at once.

"Why didn't you write? We'd had a brass band out and everything."

"I guess I have been a pretty poor writer, Major."

"Major, Major? That was ten years ago, son. I'm the judge now."

"I guess you'll always be the major to me, Dad."

Claire laughed with tears sparkling in her eyes. "To everyone else as well, Webb. It makes him so mad when they won't call him judge."

There were tears in Nadell's eyes, too, and he had to clear his throat to speak again, saying they'd get the buggy immediately and start for home. As they all turned to cross the street toward the stables, a handsome lacquered brougham was driven across in front of them and stopped at the hitch rack. Webb saw that it was Emery Bandine driving. Save for his towering size, he hardly looked the same man. He was immaculately tailored in kerseymere trousers and a rust-colored frock coat. Even his shaggy red mane was trimmed to a civilized length, its edges barely showing beneath a cream-colored Stetson that must have cost him $100. He had not seen them in the shadow of the arcade until he stopped. There was a deep aloofness in his manner as he removed his hat to Claire, nodded greeting to the men.

"Looks like everybody's celebrating a homecoming now," he said. "You remember my daughter, Webb."

He shifted as he spoke, so that Webb got his first full look at the girl sitting on Bandine's left. He remembered her as the curly-headed tot who had entranced anyone who saw her. It was a distinct shock to see her so grown up. She had on something white, that was frothy here, and clinging there, and gave a dozen tantalizing hints of the firm-breasted body beneath. Her hair was yellow as sunlight, pulled together behind the ears by a blue ribbon, and then flared out into a heavy roll across the nape of her neck. There was a reaching out and a wonderful shining innocence to her great blue eyes. It brought a sudden throb of blood through Webb's temples that he had not felt in a long time. He bowed, almost in embarrassment, murmuring a greeting.

When the major spoke, there was a noticeable reserve to his tone: "What brings the Bandines to town on such a hot day?"

"We've come in to buy my dress for the party," Kit said. "Dad promised me a regular cotillion for my first summer home from school. I do hope all of you can make it."

Webb saw the muscles freeze in Bandine's face. It made him realize that the man had not intended any such thing. The major, too, stiffened perceptibly. Kit must have sensed something wrong in the brittle silence. As she realized the mistake she had made, she showed a faint embarrassment, then her lips took on a pouting shape.

"Dad," she said in a chiding way.

It broke the tension. The major cleared his throat, forcing a chuckle. "Well," he said dryly, "I guess the cat's out of the bag."

Some of the color left Bandine's cheeks. "It's not that. I thought that with the Morales trial still in the air, and all the other trouble. . . ."

"We all know what the trouble is, and how far back it goes," Nadell said. "If it would be less awkward for all concerned, we will decline, with genuine regrets. . . ."

"Not at all," Kit protested. "Why should it be that way? I want my homecoming to be a happy one. I've grown up under this cloud, and I'm tired of it. I couldn't play with that girl when I was six because she was the daughter of a Unionist. I couldn't go to this girl's party when I was nine because her father had voted for Davis. Maybe those things were important then, but they're in the past now. The war's been over twelve years, Dad, the Reconstruction is gone. You have no reason for quarreling any more. I know we all feel badly about Morales, but the major was trying just as hard as you were to get him out of it."

"Your little girl's grown up in that year back East," Nadell said admiringly. Then he stepped over to the brougham, putting a hand on the rail. "And I think she's right, Emery. I've wanted to bury the hatchet for a long time. You know that from the beginning it was my greatest dream to bring peace back to Texas. There are still so many problems to be solved, and we can do it so much better standing together."

Bandine stared long and thoughtfully at the dashboard, with the dark reserve gradually lifting from his face. Then a droll smile touched his lips and disappeared, and he said: "I could never deny my daughter anything, Major. A Republican and a Democrat drinking in the same house will probably be the end of Texas as we know it, but you are welcome on one condition."

Nadell's face clouded. "And what is the condition?"

"That you don't try to confiscate any of my cattle for your commissary."

They all burst out laughing at that, and, when he could control his chuckling, Nadell bowed his iron-gray head and accepted the condition. They were all still laughing as Bandine helped his daughter out of the brougham, bowed to them, and took his leave. Claire saw how closely Webb was following Kit's figure with his eyes, as she accompanied her father up the street. Webb felt his sister move in beside him, speaking in a voice too low for the major to catch.

"We've forgiven you a lot, Webb. But not Kit. Please not Kit. We could never forgive you that."

In the days following Webb's return the major was too overjoyed at having his son back to probe for specific details of Webb's life during those lost years. He was quite content with Webb's colorful stories of mining camps and boom towns, and Webb's hints that now he was ready to settle down. Claire had a good idea of what Webb's life had really been, but she knew any true revelation would only hurt her father, without serving any purpose. To her, it was obvious that Webb's wanderlust was even more deeply instilled in him, and that he would be leaving soon. Her only hope was that the illusion could be maintained for her father's sake while Webb was here.

She did not worry about it as much as she might have, for her mind was too filled with Bandine. The invitation to Kit's party had given her the soaring hope that the barriers were at last gone between her and Bandine, and that her long wait would soon be over. The cotillion came on a Saturday, two weeks after the meeting in town, and Claire and her father and brother all rode out together in the family buggy.

The gambrel roof and dormer windows of the Bandine house rose out of the brasada like the topgallants of a ship, and the music of an orchestra from San Antonio was wafted out through a myriad of windows blooming with yellow light. Bandine and Kit met them at the door. He had on a scissor-tail coat, bottle green and tailored impeccably to his great-shouldered frame. His high white collar made the mahogany color of his face even darker. Kit's cheeks were filled with an excited glow, and Claire saw how her eyes immediately met Webb's and clung there.

Claire removed her broché shawl, handing it to a servant. Her moiré overskirt shimmered like silver, caught up at the sides with rosette flounces, and the neck of her green basque was cut sinfully low, leaving her bare shoulders to shine like alabaster in the light of a hundred candles. She saw Bandine's eyes grow wide, and he bowed low.

"Ma'am," he breathed. "This is enough to make me vote the straight Republican ticket."

Nadell chuckled in self-conscious pleasure. Then the greetings began. Jerry Waggoner and Hammond Innes and countless others, all looking a little surprised to find Nadell here, showed him the utmost courtesy. It made Claire realize more than ever what respect her father had gained from both parties, and she knew a deep pride in him.

Finally Bandine pulled her away from the laughing crowd and she found herself spun onto the dance floor, where a dozen couples already whirled. It was something she had dreamed of for years, something she had thought would never come. There was a trembling excitement in her, like a schoolgirl on her first date. Bandine was staring intently into her face, his voice a little husky.

"You're beautiful, Claire."

She gave him a slow smile. "Mixing with that crowd in Austin has given you polish, Emery. A few years ago you would have compared me with a spotted pup under a yaller wagon."

He threw back his head to laugh at that. She had never seen him so gay. All the dark moods the brush had molded into him seemed driven away. But despite his laughter, his droll comments, she sensed a strange undercurrent in him. More than once, over the sumptuous dinner, she caught him watching her with a somber, wondering expression on his face. And as they danced again, there were half a dozen times when his laughter suddenly ceased, the same look returned to him, and he seemed about to say something, only to check himself. It puzzled her, filled her with the sense of something about to happen, yet she did not know exactly what. It was late when they finally drifted onto the gallery. The far corner was shadowed and swimming with the scent of jasmine. They stood there in silence, watching the dancers still on the floor. Kit and Webb were swinging around and around, her eyes fixed worshipfully on his face.

"Kit seems quite smitten with your brother," Bandine said.

She sighed regretfully. "He has a way with women."

"Too much of a way. I wish you'd keep him away from my daughter, ma'am."

She stirred to look up at him and he turned quickly to her, contrition all over his face. "I'm sorry, I didn't mean to put it that way. . . ."

"Never mind," she said without anger. "I know what Webb is."

"He's not really bad, ma'am."

"No, he's merely weak. But a weak man with a flair for women can do cruel things to them."

"Then you'll help me. You'll keep him away from Kit. I think they've been seeing each other. I haven't said anything yet. I didn't want to spoil these first days at home. But I can't let it go

156

on. I can't have her hurt."

"I'll do what I can, Emery. I know how much Kit means to you."

He bowed his head, the lines graven deep at the edges of his lips. "More than ever these last years. Sometimes it seems like Kit is the only one really close to me. It's like sunshine in a room when she's there."

"Nobody can know her without loving her, Emery. She's so exquisite, so like Catherine. . . ." She broke off as he glanced sharply at her. Then she touched his arm. "I didn't mean to hurt you."

"Of course you didn't. I wasn't even thinking of that. It only shows. . . ." He trailed off, frowning, hands opening and closing, as if trying to find the right words. "What I mean is . . . Catherine being on our minds like that. You said once there were so many things standing between us. Were you thinking of Catherine, too?"

He had turned to face her, the scents of tobacco and whiskey on him a barely discernible fragrance that was somehow intensely masculine, stirring her deeply. She felt her face turning up toward his.

"Isn't it true, Emery?"

He caught her bare arms. His hands felt hot against her flesh. "I've been wanting to talk about it all evening. I can cuss a man out or talk every day about cattle. But when it comes to saying what I feel, it's so hard. . . ."

She began to realize fully what he wanted to say, and felt a distinct shock. Could she expect so much all at once? It was difficult for her to speak.

"Maybe I can help you, Emery. We all know how much you loved Catherine. Maybe it would take you longer to get over her death than an ordinary man. But Dad told me time would heal it, sooner or later."

"After that kiss in the courthouse, I felt like I'd betrayed Catherine somehow."

"But now you know that's wrong. You've had enough time to see it in its true light. Catherine will always be a part of your life that no other woman can have. You still love her, Emery, and you always will. But not as a living woman. You still have another part of your life to fulfill, and you won't betray Catherine by doing it. She'd be the first one to tell you that."

"You're saying all the things I've tried to tell myself. It's been so mixed up in me. But it sounds right now." He was speaking swiftly, intensely, as if her nearness this evening had at last released all the hungers and needs bottled up in him so long by the grip of Catherine's memory. "I should have seen that a long time ago. Maybe if I hadn't been so busy scrambling for my kids, we could have found out."

Her face was turned up to him, her eyes almost closed. "It's not too late, Emery."

His hands tightened on her arms till it hurt. He drew her against him and dipped his head to kiss her. A roaring filled her head. She lost all measurement of time. When he finally pulled away, a deep tremor ran through her body.

"This house has been too long without a woman, Claire. Will you come to it?" His voice shook a little. "Will you marry me?"

Her eyes were still closed, hiding the tears. "Yes," she said softly. "I'll marry you, Emery."

XVII

Bandine and Claire made no announcement to the gathering that evening. She wanted him to be sure that it had not been just the spell of the night, that he was truly free of all the barriers that had stood between them. He thought about it those next days but found no doubts in him. A few years ago, even a month ago, he would not have believed that two loves could exist in him. But now he was beginning to realize that many loves actually lay side by side in a man—the love of his friends, his children, his land, his woman—each related to the other, yet standing separate and distinct. He finally could not wait longer, and rode over to ask Nadell formally for his daughter's hand. Nadell showed his wry smile and made some jokes about ruining the two-party system in the United States, and gave his wholehearted permission. Then Bandine rode back home and got Adah and Kit and Rusty into the library and broke the news. Kit rushed to him and threw her arms about his neck, kissing him and crying and laughing all at once.

"A man needs a woman." Adah beamed. "And there's none finer than Claire."

"We can make it a double wedding," Kit said.

"A double wedding?"

The smile left her face. She looked confused. "I'd meant to tell you, Dad. Webb and I. . . ."

"Webb!"

His sharp tone jerked her head up. "Yes," she said. "We want to get married."

"Kit, you can't be serious, you're not sixteen. . . ."

"You married Mother when she was that old."

"But not Webb. You know what he is, Kit. A gambler, a drifter, a shiftless parasite."

"Dad, stop! He's Claire's brother. You ask our approval of her and turn around and talk like this about him. I won't listen to a lot of malicious lies."

"Kit, I forbid you. . . ."

"You can't stop me, Dad. I'm going to marry Webb."

She ran out of the room and upstairs and they could hear her sobbing all the way. Bandine stood in a deep and helpless frustration, the pulse in his neck throbbing. Adah started to say something, but, when she saw the stony anger in his face, she lifted a corner of her apron to tear-filled eyes and went back to the kitchen. Rusty remained in silent disapproval by the table.

"I suppose you're against me, too."

"Nobody's against you, Dad. What Webb is doesn't particularly matter. If you'd only show Kit a little more understanding."

"What kind of understanding? Let her marry the fool? Let her ruin her life? It was my fault not to nip it in the bud." The hurt and anger filled Bandine so roughly that he had no control over the way his words tumbled out. "And while we're on the subject, we'd better stop something else before it gets this bad. Seems like you're spending all your time in town now. Come home at dawn, sleep till noon." He wheeled to the sideboard, pulled open a drawer, got a scrap of paper from it, and handed it to Rusty. "One of the I.O.U.s you gave Samuels. He said he'd held it as long as he could. You want to gamble, you should at least learn how to play poker."

The boy flushed, staring doggedly down at the chit. Bandine paced across the room. "I don't mind you hanging around that saloon or playing cards. But you can't spend all your time there. That's what happened to Webb. It's time you got out in the brush and learned your trade."

The boy's head sank lower. "You know it didn't do any good the last time I tried, Dad."

"You had bad luck. You're older now. . . ."

"And I want to be a lawyer more than ever."

"Why?" Bandine struck the table. "Your whole family comes out of the brasada, Rusty. You belong there. The Double Bit is yours. Who's going to run it after I'm gone?"

The boy shook his head. "Please, Dad, we've gone over that so many times. I just know it's not for me. I'm no good at it and I don't want it."

"You don't know any such thing. You're as bad as Kit. You're too young to be so set on anything. Maybe I'm rushing you. In a year or so you'll be old enough to realize you belong to the cattle business. I'm willing to give you the rope, Rusty, but don't hang yourself with it. I won't let you turn out like Webb Nadell. If these chits keep coming in, I'm going to drag you out by your heels every time I catch you in that saloon."

Those next days were bitterly frustrating for Bandine. Whenever he tried to talk with Kit about Webb, it ended in a battle, and finally she began locking herself in her room when he was home. Both Bandine and Claire tried to argue Webb out of it, but he gave them no satisfaction at all. It put a great blight on what Claire and Bandine had found together, and left Bandine in a black mood.

The Double Bit needed some new strings for fall beef roundup, so on the next horse day Bandine rode into town with his foreman, George Remington. The corrals west of the river were full of horses and half the countryside had come in to trade and buy. Bandine took little interest in it, however, standing gloomily around the cook fires with a cup of coffee and letting Remington handle things. The trading went on till after nightfall, but finally Bandine grew so restless that he started for O'Hara's place, hoping a drink would relax him. The saloonkeeper was on a ladder, lighting the kerosene torches on the overhang of his building. They flared up and shot their ruddy illumination into the street, puddling it with miniature lakes of yellow fire.

The inside was already crowded, fogged with blue tobacco smoke, the long bar lined two deep with drinkers. Bandine shouldered in between a pair of cowpunchers and got his beer. His eyes lifted idly to the backbar mirror as he drank. The card tables on the other side of the room were reflected in the glass. At one, he saw Dan Holichek, Ewing Samuels, Webb Nadell, a hostler, and Rusty, playing stud. It filled him with such a shock of anger he almost gagged on his drink.

They had not seen him, and he moved down through the crowd till he could follow the play. Webb Nadell was dealing, with his back to Bandine. But his hands were visible, and Bandine found himself temporarily fascinated by the supple skill of his long pale fingers. Rusty was the obvious winner in the game, with a big pile of gold eagles and chips before him. Bandine could not quite understand a man with Webb's skill allowing a boy to take the play away from him so completely, and it made him suspicious.

The first cards were dealt, one to a man, face down all around. Webb dealt the second round. This one was face up, an ace for Rusty, a ten for Webb, miscellaneous small numbers for the other men. Being ace-high, Rusty put out a big bet. Webb raised him and Rusty took the bait, raising back. It was too rich for the others and they began dropping out. Finally it was only Rusty and Webb, raising each other till Rusty had put most of his winnings into the pot. Then he called, and Webb picked up the deck to deal the third card.

Bandine saw how he held it—three fingers on one side, the index finger on top, the thumb at the upper corner of the deck— and in that instant Bandine knew how he had set it up. He had run into more than one center dealer in the deadfalls at Abilene. Webb had undoubtedly fed Rusty an ace for his down card. The boy, with two aces against Webb's ten that was showing, had naturally bet high. And now Webb was set for the killing. Bandine moved away from the bar, in behind Webb, as the man dealt to Rusty. The boy's eyes were on the card, and he did not see Bandine. It was a seven, and Bandine saw disappointment take all the air out of Rusty. Before Webb could deal his own card, Bandine reached over and pinned his wrist to the table, the deck beneath his hand.

"A thousand dollars your card is a ten, Webb."

The noise of the room died suddenly. The men were used to the message of trouble, and Bandine's voice had carried it to the farthest corner. There was a strained tension to the line of Webb's neck as he stared up at Bandine.

"You haven't got any right to horn in," Holichek said.

"Stay out of this," Bandine told him. "I just hope you ain't in on it. Is it a bet, Webb?"

The pain of Bandine's grip on Webb's wrist was showing in his face. Slowly he let his pinned fingers spread away from the deck, allowed Bandine to pull his hand off. Bandine turned the top card over. It was a ten. Bandine turned Webb's down card up. It was a ten, also, giving him three of them. Bandine leaned over and flipped Rusty's down card up. It was an ace. Bandine straightened up, knowing he didn't have to say anything. Webb's three tens would have topped Rusty's pair of aces. It would have escaped notice in the ordinary run of the game, but now that it was exposed, there were enough men in the crowd who had seen a center dealer work before. A sullen murmur began to run through them, like the growl of an animal in its cage.

Bandine caught Webb by his lapels, pulling him out of the chair till he was standing on his toes. Webb's whole weight hung against Bandine's grip. His arms were slack and he made no move to struggle.

"If I find you in this town tomorrow," Bandine said, "I'll take a horsewhip to you."

The man did not answer. No expression showed on his face. It was as gray, as waxen as a dead man's, with the eyes fixed emptily on Bandine. The sense of being unable to reach him angered Bandine even more, and he flung Webb from him. The gambler staggered backward into one of the men sitting at another table, almost falling. He dragged himself erect and stood with stooped shoulders, the hollows beneath his cheek bones turned cavernous by shadows cast from the overhead lights. A thin rancor brought a yellow tinge to his eyes, and then faded again, as he continued to stare at Bandine. With a curse Bandine turned to Rusty.

"Get up. We're getting out of here."

The boy did not move. His eyes were fixed on Bandine's face, smoldering and black. Bandine circled Samuels to catch the boy's arm, jerking him bodily out of the chair and shoving him toward the door. Rusty stumbled into the dense crowd at the bar. But Bandine was going right behind, and the men spread to let the two of them through. Bandine followed Rusty out the door and they stopped momentarily on the walk.

"We're going home."

The expression on the boy's face checked Bandine. All the planes of it seemed compressed, the lips pinched tightly, the eyes squinted as if in pain.

"Damn you," the boy said. "Damn you . . . !"

He broke off and whirled and ran off the sidewalk, tearing his bridle reins free from the rack and jumping aboard his horse. He backed it into the street and spurred it in a dead run out of town. Bandine watched him go, sick at his stomach and utterly helpless. The sullen roar of the crowd grew from within the saloon, and Webb was pushed through the batwing doors. He stumbled and almost fell. He checked himself a moment, glancing at Bandine, with that thin rancor in his face, and then turned to walk down the street. Bandine hardly saw him, still watching his son run out of town. Finally, however, he became aware of Holichek, standing just outside the door, and turned toward the man.

"What else did you expect?" Holichek said. "What would you do if somebody humiliated you like that, in front of the whole town?"

"Humiliated, hell! I just kept Rusty from losing his shirt. You all saw what Webb was doing to him. You know how a center dealer works."

"What's the difference what Webb was doing? You treated Rusty like a little kid. You showed him up before everybody. You couldn't have humiliated him more. You'll be lucky if he don't run out on you."

Bandine wheeled away, too miserable to feel anger at Holichek. He walked blindly down the street, needing some escape from the confused hurt in him. It had been such a natural impulse to protect his son, to prove to him what kind of men he was befriending. Why couldn't the boy see that? Everything he did seemed wrong. It was like an immense pressure building up in him. He suddenly felt that, if he didn't find some escape, he would come apart at the seams. He turned into the first saloon he reached. It went back to the old days, when he had come in after roundup, the pressures of loneliness and heartbreaking labor too great to be born without some release.

The rest of that night was lost in alcoholic haze. He knew he broke a row of windows somewhere, shot somebody's mirror to shards, drove somebody's buggy and team through a fence of the horse corral, and ended up in an upstairs room of the inn. Then, out of the haze, there were shots, half a dozen of them, a whole round from a six-gun. Poppa Lockwood, running into the room, stared at the rungs Bandine had shot out of the foot of the iron bedstead. Bandine was lying down and sticking his feet through the opening he had created.

"They must've made these beds for midgets. I'm tired of sleeping all folded up like a jackknife every time I come to town."

When he awoke the next noon, he was sick and disgusted and it had not helped. He gave Poppa a blank check and asked him to pay all the damages he had caused in town. Then he rode home. He got there late at night, and the lights in the dining room gave him his first premonition. He found Adah in there, eyes red from crying.

"It's Kit," Adah told him. "She's run off to be married with Webb Nadell."

XVIII

That autumn was the longest Claire Nadell had ever spent. She and Bandine had not planned to get married till late in the year, for the fence cutting was still a bitter issue, and the roundup would be a hard one, needing all Bandine's attention. But Kit's elopement had hit him hard, and, even during the time Claire could see Bandine, it lay like a shadow over their happiness. Finally September came, and Bandine disappeared into the brush with his crews.

Claire knew that it was his way to throw himself into the labors in an effort to rid himself of the black mood Kit's loss had left. He came back for good in October, gaunt and tired and burned almost black by the sun.

They heard from Kit that month, too. The postmark was from Julesburg, but she said they were not living there, and would not tell her father where to find them, for fear he would come after her. This only enraged him more, and he was in no state to discuss the wedding for weeks. But finally they set the date for the 15th of November.

For a week the Nadell kitchen was like a beehive. The ovens were hot twenty-four hours a day, with the scent of baking bread and fruitcake and pound cake filling the whole lower floor. In the smoke-blackened fireplaces of the cavernous kitchen were spitted quarters of beef and whole pigs and rows of opossums brought in by every neighbor boy for miles around.

The first frost came on the night of the 14th and Claire awoke on her wedding day to look out on a land covered with a million Christmas trees. Pearl came up to help with her hair. Soon the guests began to arrive, and all during the time Pearl worked at the finger puffs, the jingle of bits and stamp of horses floated up through the windows. Then came the dress.

The bustles that had replaced hoops in the early 'Seventies were growing smaller each year, and Pearl spent an interminable time draping the overskirt to her satisfaction. At last she stepped away, black, amplitudinous, grinning triumphantly at the shimmering sheath of the satin bodice, clinging so tightly to the fullness of Claire's upper body.

"Hard to tell which is snowier, honey, you or that satin."

Claire smiled nervously, then wheeled to stare out at the lines of buggies and hacks at the hitching rings. "Has Emery come yet?"

Pearl giggled. "You asked me that a dozen times already. He done come an hour ago. Down there drinking and making jokes with your father. And just as scaired as you."

There was a furtive knock on the door. Pearl opened it a crack. It was Leander, her gawky son, eyes wide and frightened in his black face.

"It's Mastah Webb," he said. "He come up the back way. He wants to see you in his room."

Claire's heart seemed to stop. For a moment her mind was completely blank with shock. Then, unwilling to speculate on why he should come this way, she gathered up her skirt and followed Pearl. Webb would have been seen from below if he had come to Claire's room. It must have been why he had stopped at his room, around the turn in the hall. The same thing made Pearl keep her bulk between the balcony rail and Claire, so that the groom would have no chance of seeing his bride too soon. Webb was pacing in front of the windows when Pearl opened the door. His face was white and pinched about the mouth, his clothes rumpled and travel-stained. Pearl stayed outside, and Claire closed the door. Her brother walked swiftly to her, catching her hands.

"Honey, this is a terrible way to arrive for your wedding. . . ."

"Webb, what's happened?"

He let her go, wheeled around, walking back to the window. He licked his lips, rubbed his hands together, glared out through the leaded glass.

"I need your help, Sis. I was afraid to come back. But I'm dead broke and I couldn't get any farther. . . ."

"Why should you be afraid to come back?" She walked to him, dropping her skirts, clutching his arm. "Webb, what are you trying to say. Where's Kit?"

He put his hands on the window sill, gripping it so tightly the knuckles shone translucently through the pale flesh. A sobbing sound racked his voice.

"Kit . . . Kit . . . she's dead. . . ."

He broke off, head bowed deeply. Claire was so stunned she could not react in any way. All the blood drained from her cheeks, leaving them white as her dress. Webb shut his eyes and bit his lips. Then, with a sudden wheeling motion, he went over to the bed and sat down, head dropped into his hands.

"I couldn't help it, Sis. She was sick. It was so cold up there. She was sick and I'd lost my job and we had a fight."

She stared at him a long time, before she could bring the words out. "Sick with what?"

He shook his head savagely from side to side. "I don't know. The doctor said pneumonia, when I saw him again. . . ."

"*Again?* Do you mean you left her?"

"I didn't know how bad it was, Claire, or I wouldn't have done it for the world. . . ."

She walked swiftly to him and grasped his shoulders, shaking him. "Webb, what are you saying? Do you mean you left her while she was sick?"

He pulled her hands off and held them in his own, looking up at her with an intense agitation in his pale wedge of a face.

"Claire, I didn't mean it, you've got to believe me. I wouldn't have done it for the world. . . ."

The look on her face stopped him. She pulled away from him. He caught at her hands again, stumbling to his feet. Sweat had broken out on his sallow forehead, giving it a greasy shine. His words became slurred, his voice shrill with plea.

"Sis, please, I didn't know this was your wedding day. I had no idea Emery would be here. You'll tell him about Kit. I can't. He'd kill me. You know he would. Just a little money, Sis. I wouldn't have done it for the world, you know I wouldn't. I can get out the back way. . . ."

"Then you'd better go."

His eyes were blank. "But you've got to help me."

"I've been helping you all my life, Webb." She was sick, deeply sick, and her voice had a dead sound. "I've lied to Dad for you, perpetuated your little illusions, forgiven you the countless people you've hurt, overlooked your meanness and your shallowness. I'll never do it again. When you leave this house, it will be for the last time."

He tried to catch at her hands again, but checked himself at the sound of voices from outside. The stairway was shaking to the heavy pound of feet. Someone called Claire's name.

"It's Emery," she said. "Samuels must have told him."

Webb went white. He opened his mouth, but no sound came out. In that last instant the habits and ties of a lifetime asserted themselves, and Claire knew that despite her resolve to be finished with Webb she had to prevent Bandine from finding him here. She knew Bandine's rage, knew him quite capable of killing Webb if he found this out, and could not deliberately expose her brother to that, even now. She turned and opened the door and stepped out, closing it behind her. Bandine was at the head of the stairs. He halted a moment, staring blankly at her, face flushed with the exertion of running upstairs. Then he called: "Samuels said he saw Webb. Did he bring Kit?"

She began to walk down the balcony. "Webb's already left, Emery."

He started toward her, frowning at the expression on her face. She knew it was still pale and set; she couldn't help that. He began to walk toward her.

"Claire, you're lying to me. Why did you stay in his room if he's left?"

He had reached her and she caught his arm, trying gently to turn him. "Come to my room, Emery."

He refused to be wheeled aside. "Webb's still in his room, isn't he? Something's happened. I can see it in your face. What's he hiding for?" He abruptly quit trying to get around her, as the thought struck him. He caught her arms. His voice shook as he spoke. "Is it Kit?"

The pain of his grip was so great that she fought involuntarily to twist free. "Emery, please. . . ."

"Is she sick? Did he leave her somewhere?"

"Emery, you're hurting me . . . !"

He released her just as suddenly as he had grasped her. He stepped back. His cheeks were a putty color; his eyes looked sunken and blank with shock. She knew it was what her face must have looked like when she first heard about Kit.

"She's dead," he said. His voice was painfully strained, barely audible. "I can see it in your face. Webb wouldn't be afraid to see me for any other reason. Kit's dead."

With one hand she was holding her throbbing right arm. "Emery, if you'll just come to my room. . . ."

He made an inarticulate sound and tried to rush by her. She caught at him, almost torn off balance by his rush, hanging on him with all her weight.

"He killed her," Bandine said hoarsely. "He wouldn't be hiding for any other reason. . . ."

"Emery, don't go in there . . . !"

"I'll kill him, Claire. Let me go. I swear I'll kill him!"

She saw the terrible, wounded rage turning his eyes blank, and knew he could not be stopped once he got his hands on Webb. She threw all her weight against him in her struggle to stop him. He tried to twist her free and it swung him around into the banister. She heard the crash of breaking wood as his great weight fell heavily into the flimsy railing. It broke and his body pitched over into the sea of upturned faces below. Claire was almost pulled with him, but she caught the remains of the banister in the last instant. She had a dizzy glimpse of his body sprawled on the floor below.

As she turned to run downstairs, she saw Webb dart from his room. He stopped at the broken banister, looking down at Bandine. Then he wheeled and ran for the back stairs.

Claire hurried down to the first floor, elbowing through the people packed around Bandine. They had helped him to a sitting position against the wall. Pain squinted his eyes, and his face was beaded with sweat. The major and a couple of other men were trying to lift him.

"Get him on the couch. . . ."

Bandine groaned in pain, fighting off their pawing hands. "Don't move me," he said. "My leg's broke all to hell."

XIX

The winter of 1877 was the worst Spanish Crossing had known in twenty years. It was the year of the big drifts. Sleet came in November, snow in December. And ice in January, lying like a sheet over the ground, covering the graze for hundreds of miles. In their blind search for warmth and grass the cattle began to drift. They came like the buffalo, from as far north as Oklahoma and Kansas, driven before the blizzards in masses so vast no man could estimate their numbers. They pushed into Frío

County and drove the local herds before them, traveling inevitably southward.

A drift fence might have stopped them, but a year of fence cutting lay before this winter, and there were few whole fences standing. The riders could not turn them back, for there were too many, and they were being driven before a herd instinct as old as time.

And when it was over, and the crews from Frío County had to ride as far south as the Gulf coast to cut their cattle out of the herds that had drifted there, they found pitifully few left under their brand. For thousands had been trampled to death or had frozen or starved on the march. It was a blow that brought many of the big operators to their knees. But it was a boon to the Holichek brothers.

Big Bob swept into town on one of his flying visits that March, with the usual telegram ahead of time to insure a welcoming committee. There was the invariable round of cigars, the sly implications of big things at Austin, the drink left half finished at the bar—then Dan was closeted upstairs with his brother. Bob was getting a tremendous paunch, and wheezed with the effort of slightest movement.

"Why don't you get decent heat in this hole? Hasn't changed in twenty years." He stamped officiously around the room, blowing on his hands to warm them. He then asked about Bandine. Lighting the cast-iron stove, Dan told Bob that the winter had hit Bandine even worse than the others. His broken leg had kept him from joining his crews in their attempt to stop the drifts. Bob asked about the marriage, saying they would lose everything if Bandine became Nadell's son-in-law. Dan said Bandine had not seen Claire since the ill-fated wedding day. Bob chuckled, tramping to the stove, lifting up his coattails to warm his hams.

"I guess not," he said. "I guess Bandine couldn't marry the

172

girl when her brother killed his daughter. Not Bandine." He shook his head, grinning slyly. "And Nadell?"

"He's agreed to run on our ticket. I've convinced him we'll back him on everything he asks."

Bob chuckled triumphantly. "You're almost as good a liar as me, Dan. Nadell's name will have us in power again for sure. Might even run him for governor next year." He frowned, dropping the coattails. "Only one thing standing in our way, then. What about this rumor that the big operators are putting Bandine up for state senator?"

Dan told him it was more than a rumor. One more winter like this could ruin Bandine and the other big men. The only thing that would save them were fences to stop the cattle from drifting. But they couldn't keep barbed wire up with the fence cutters at work. The big operators had to stop the fence cutting this year or they were through. And with Bandine in the senate and Waggoner in the lower house, they could really push through the bill making fence cutting a felony. Nadell wouldn't stand much chance, either, if Bandine ran against him. Big Bob shook his head, saying that mustn't happen.

"It won't," Dan said. "You know how Bandine feels about his kids. He's already lost one. He'd sell his soul to keep Rusty. I can set it up so that, if Bandine runs for senator, he'll lose his son for good. Do you think he'll run under those circumstances?"

Big Bob stared at his brother, understanding dawning slowly in his sly, pouched eyes. Then he began to chuckle. It grew to laughter, great wheezing laughter that filled the room. He sounded like a windsucker every time he drew in a breath and his cheeks puffed out and grew red and a pattern of purple whiskey veins appeared in his bulbous nose. He suddenly seemed very ugly to Dan, very ugly and bloated and corrupt. Dan turned and walked to the window, staring through the gathering steam and the dust and the flyspecks at the street below.

He was remembering that first meeting with Rusty, when he had been on his way to the gathering of the little operators—remembering that moment of rapport, when he had touched the boy. Remembering how it had disgusted him to think of using the kid. Why hadn't he kept that feeling? Why had he let himself drift into this, cultivating the boy, using the things that stood between Rusty and his father?

"Bob," he said, "give me five thousand dollars."

Big Bob almost choked on his laughter. "What?"

"I've been your boy. I've done all your grimy little jobs. You wouldn't have Spanish Crossing without me. . . ."

"What would you do with that much?"

"Send Rusty to college. He wants to be a lawyer. It's the big dream of his life. He wants to do something for those poor fools out in the brush, wants to stop all this damned fighting about nothing. He could, too, Bob. I've done a lot of dirty things, but I can't use a son against his father that way."

"You damn' fool!" Big Bob said. It stopped Dan. Bob stamped over and stood before him, breathing stertorously, frowning intensely at him. Finally he spoke disgustedly: "You know why you won't ever amount to anything, Dan?"

"That hasn't got anything. . . ."

"You're soft." Big Bob wheeled to tramp across the room, pulling a cigar from his coat. "You haven't got a pure gut in your body. You got a dozen irons in the fire, always something big going. But you never quite make it pan out, do you? Because you're little, Dan. You're small-time."

Dan Holichek's swarthy cheeks grew red; his black eyes began to dance. Big Bob stopped to pare off the end of his cigar with his penknife, chuckling maliciously.

"You hate that, don't you? When I'm not around, you think

you're the big frog here. You stand around with that cigar in your mouth and tell them how you elected Hayes and E.J. Davis and they lick your boots like it was candy. It's the breath of life to you." Bob fired up his cigar, talking between puffs. "But deep down in your heart you know. This is just a little puddle. And you're just a little frog. You know it whenever I come back. It kills you to hear them call me Big Bob, doesn't it? You're Little Dan, then. You hate my guts for it. You know you'll never be anything more than a tinhorn boss of a bunch of county stooges. You haven't got the guts to be anything else. . . ."

"Guts?" Dan said hotly. "What do you know about guts? You've never been able to stop Bandine. If he's going to be pulled down, I'll do it."

"You'll never make it, little brother."

"I will. And you'll pay a price for it this time. Not any penny-ante five thousand dollars. You're going to find a spot at the capital for me. A nice juicy plum. . . ."

"What if I agree? There's a spot in the Attorney General's office at Austin. You pull strings, you get big gravy."

It stopped Dan Holichek. He was breathing heavily. He knew exactly what Big Bob had done to him, but he couldn't help it. He said: "If I talked, even after Bandine was ruined, it would pull the whole thing down on you."

"Don't worry about me going back on my word," Big Bob said. Dan turned and walked back to the window, staring out. Big Bob wreathed himself in fragrant smoke, all affability and portly charm again. "And all that sentiment about the boy," he said. "It's over?"

It was a long time before Dan roused himself to answer. His voice had a dull sound. "I just had to have my moment," he said. "Like getting dirty. Once in a while you got to wash, even though you know you'll get dirty again, just for your own self-respect."

"Don't kid me. Who has self-respect?"

"Yeah," Dan Holichek said. "Who has self-respect?"

It was a terrible year for Bandine. His leg had been broken in two places and took months to heal, confining him to the house long into the spring. The doctor said it was because he had no will to get well. Kit's death seemed to have stunned him, leaving a bowed husk of a man who sat most of the day in the library, his leg propped up on a stool, staring blankly before him.

He really had no clear picture of what had happened to him. He only knew there was a sick pain, deep inside him, that nothing would drive out. He only knew that all desire for life seemed drained from him. He had no hunger, no want of people; his mind was utterly closed off from all the usual needs. Neither Adah nor Rusty could reach him. He wouldn't see Claire, and she knew what must be going on inside him and didn't force herself upon him. She remembered what time had done in the case of Catherine, and clung to the hope that it would be her ally now.

The spring dragged on, and his leg finally healed enough to hobble around on. He began to take a listless interest in the ordinary things of life, put some of his weight back on, found some of the old vitality returning. By fall he was riding, and joined the roundup. He could do no roping or heavy brushpopping, and spent most of his time in camp with the branding.

On the 12th of October, Waggoner rode out to tell him that the state Democratic chairman, Guthrie, was in Spanish Crossing. He would only be there one more day. They could hold up their plans no longer, and, if Bandine would not agree to run for senator, they would have to throw it to Mead. He was a weaker man, and they didn't have too much hope of Mead's defeating Nadell at the polls. But Big Bob's bunch was already starting their campaign, and the Democrats could wait no longer. Waggoner wanted Bandine to return with him that afternoon, but Bandine was still reluctant. He found himself unable to make a quick decision on anything, and thought it was Kit's death still fogging his mind. He asked Waggoner to give him more time. The man arose from the saddle he had used as a seat.

"All right, Emery. If you come in tomorrow, we'll know you've decided to run. If you don't show up, we'll assume you've decided not to."

As Waggoner mounted and turned to go, Bandine saw another rider at the edge of the thickets. It was Rusty, his town clothes filmed with dust and scarred by the brush. He greeted Waggoner as the man left, and then rode on in.

"This is the last place I'd look for you," Bandine said. "What brings you out?"

"Riding this way," Rusty said vaguely. "Thought I'd drop in and see how roundup was coming."

"Not much left to roundup, after the big drift," Bandine said. "Light down and have some coffee."

Bandine watched him dismount. The boy was almost seventeen now, already close to six feet tall, losing the bony awkwardness that had marked his adolescence. He squatted down and reached for the pot. Bandine knew a sudden stabbing need for Rusty's companionship. "Seems like a long time since I've really seen you, jigger. I guess I've been going around in a fog ever since Kit died. I guess I'm just beginning to pull out of it."

"You were a long way off," Rusty said, pouring the coffee. "None of us could reach you." He stood up, handing a cup to Bandine. He frowned, and then spoke with distinct effort. "Dad, I saw Claire the other day. Don't you think you could . . . ?"

He broke off as Bandine's head jerked up, eyes filled with a mingled rage and pain. Then Bandine turned around, took a couple of limping steps away from the fire, gripping the tin cup tightly, without even feeling the burning heat of it.

"Dad, it wasn't Claire's fault," Rusty said. "She had no control over what Webb did. I loved Kit as much as you did, but I can't see this. You have no right to go on punishing Claire for something she couldn't control. . . ."

"Punishing Claire?" It seemed torn from Bandine. "What do you think I've been going through? I've tried, Rusty. Believe me I've tried. I've told myself she isn't to blame. But Webb was her brother, Rusty. He left Kit stranded, without money, coming down with pneumonia. He might as well've taken a gun to her. I saw Nadell in town last week. I started shaking all over. I broke out in a cold sweat. I got sick to my stomach. It was his son and her brother. How can I face any of them, knowing that?"

He stopped, with the last light of day giving a gray tinge to the misery of his face, dimly highlighting the peaks of his prominent cheek bones and dropping pale shadows into the gaunt hollows beneath them. All his life he had been brought up against the blind depths of his own feelings—his intense pride, his anger, his love of his children that bordered on an obsession—and he knew now that no matter what his mind told him he was helpless before this sick rejection of anything connected with Webb Nadell. He shook his head in that characteristic gesture, like some ringy bull shaking the brush out of its horns, and turned back to Rusty.

"Let's not spoil today with it. You're all I have left now, Rusty. I don't want to fight with you any more. It's like you say, I've been away. And if I run for senator, I may be away again."

"Is that what Waggoner was here for?"

"Yes. I've got to decide tomorrow."

"That's what he meant when he said they'd know you'd

decided to run if they saw you in town tomorrow. And if you get elected, you'll put through the bill making fence cutting a felony. And if it's made a felony, Santero's appeal won't have a chance."

"That's one of the things that's held me back. But Waggoner says that after the bill is passed, we can get Santero off on a technicality. He was involved in that fence cutting before it was made a felony."

"What if he can't get Santero off?"

Bandine shook his head in angry confusion. "But he can. He told me so."

"But what if he can't? You refuse to face it, don't you? I've been up to see Santero at Huntsville, Dad. You know how old he is. He can't take this. If he doesn't get that appeal, he won't live another year. He's a broken man. You're taking a chance on Waggoner's word when it might mean Santero's life. . . ."

"You're twisting this all around," Bandine snapped. "Waggoner knows how I feel about Santero. He wouldn't take a chance on the old man. We're up against the wall, jigger. If fence cutting isn't made a felony this year, we won't have a thing to fight with. We'll be through."

"How many times have I heard that before?"

"And each time it was true. Only now a hundred times more so. . . ."

"So it boils down to the fact that you'll sacrifice Santero to save yourself."

"Not myself, jigger, can't you see that?"

"You're talking about doing it all for me again. I couldn't live in your house if it was bought with Santero's suffering, Dad. If you go into town tomorrow, I'm leaving for good!"

XX

Dan Holichek usually rose about 10:00 in the morning, washed in his hotel room, trimmed his spade beard, and ate at the inn. All during breakfast he was aware of something unusual stirring the town. Riders were constantly trotting past the inn, kicking up so much dust that it filtered inside and started Holichek coughing over his last cup of coffee. He paid Poppa Lockwood and went outside for his morning cigar. Over the roof top of the Martinez house, on the high land west of town, the old Spanish jail was visible. The horsemen were gathering there, with John Friar in their midst, his sheriff's badge winking in the bright sunlight.

While Holichek pared his cigar, O'Hara came from his saloon to observe the unusual movement through Cabildo, his thumbs tucked complacently into flowered galluses. As Holichek started across the street, Harry Geddings came from the door of the cheap hotel where he roomed, hobbling toward First Street where he could turn up to join the group before the jail. He was not the same man he had been before the bullet crippled him out in the brush. He had lost twenty pounds and his hair was snow white. His look of thick-bodied competence was gone; he stood stooped and hollow-chested, his face seamed with bitterness. He saw Holichek coming and stopped by O'Hara, speaking with a trembling rancor in his voice.

"You'll see the end of it now, Holichek. Friar's got fifty men in that posse. He'll have more when Innes and the others join him with their crews. Why don't you go out and join the fence cutters now?"

"Geddings," Holichek said mildly, "you know I never had anything to do with the fence cutters. What's all the fuss about?"

Geddings glared at him with squinted, disbelieving eyes, then spat it out: "You know's well as I. If Bandine reaches the senate, fence cutting is certain to be made a felony. Everybody knows that, if he shows up here today, he means to run for office. The fence cutters are just waiting for that. The minute he hits town, they claim they'll pull down every inch of wire in a hundred miles. But they won't even get started. Friar'll be out there waiting for 'em. One move toward a fence and this county will go up in smoke. I just wish I could be out there with Friar. I just wish I could catch that Santero cutting a fence once more."

He spat at the curb, gripping his cane till his knuckles looked like shiny knobs. Then he wheeled and hobbled on down the street, shaking the whole walk with the thump of his cane. Holichek turned to O'Hara, black brows raised. "Looks like a showdown."

"It does, at that," O'Hara said.

Holichek smiled blandly at him. He felt a distaste in O'Hara, felt that the man had evaluated him a long time ago and disliked what he had found. It was sort of a tacit, armed truce between them, for O'Hara had maintained a professional neutrality in this town for twenty years which neither wars nor politics could affect, and this was merely another eddy in the stream for him. His Irish face was completely enigmatic as he went back inside. Holichek glanced idly down the street to see that Friar's men were not the only ones in town. Billy Graves idled with a couple of Mexicans in front of the stables, their dark faces intent on the street, and farther down were more men out of the brush, standing by a water trough. The fence cutters would know as soon as Bandine went up to see Guthrie.

Holichek went into the saloon and found Henry Tevis at the front end of the bar with a beer. He halted there, asking the man: "Rusty all primed?"

Tevis glanced covertly toward the rear, where Rusty and Garrison and Revere sat at a deal table. "He come in last night, all upset after another fight with his dad. I think he's ready for you now, Dan."

Holichek walked back and slid in beside Rusty. The boy's clothes were rumpled and caked with dust, his face white and pinched around the lips.

"How's everything?" Holichek asked. "Your dad going to run for the senate?"

Rusty's voice sounded strained. "I told him I'd leave him if he did."

Holichek studied the burning intensity of the boy's eyes, the square and stubborn shape of his underlip, realizing that this was the culmination toward which he had been working so long. It had been no great problem to cultivate Rusty, through the years. It had been merely a matter of following the natural drift of things. Holichek had none of the inarticulateness that so often blocked Bandine off from reaching Rusty. Talk was his greatest commodity. He had seen the needs in the boy, had been able to draw him out, touching his interests, fulfilling them. He had spent many hours over his law books with Rusty, had gone fishing with him, had included him as an equal in the group at the saloon, until it was natural for Rusty to identify himself closely with them. And since so many of them were allied with the brushpoppers, it had taken little effort to push Rusty one step farther into the camp of the fence cutters. It had been a natural result of the things already shaping the boy's life—his friendship for Santero, going so far back, the gulf between him and his father growing steadily broader.

As he studied Rusty, Holichek felt a vague resurgence of the self-disgust he had known the last time with Big Bob. But there were stronger needs at work in him now. The thought of Austin had been constantly in his mind, driving him, and he had refused to let the sentiment over Rusty reach him fully again.

"Where would you go," he asked Rusty, "if you left your father?"

"To us," Revere said. "Where else?"

"You mean this fence cutting?"

"That's right," Revere said. "The fences are what give the big men power. Why else would they fight so hard to keep them? Cut the fences and we destroy the power. Do that and they won't be able to put Bandine in the senate. Fence cutting will not become a felony, and Santero's appeal will go through. You told us that yourself."

"Did I?" mused Holichek. "It sounds logical." He studied his cigar. "They gathering at Santero's?"

"Mexican Thickets."

Holichek glanced at Rusty. "And you ride with them?"

Rusty nodded miserably. "If Dad comes to town, I will. He's got to be stopped some way, Dan. He's got to be shown."

Before Holichek answered, Billy Graves appeared at the door, calling softly. Holichek knew what it was, and rose and went quickly to the door, pushing through. He heard Rusty's chair scrape back, heard the boy's boots against the floor.

The horseman was coming alone from the south end of Cabildo, a towering figure in the saddle, the sun flaming on the shaggy edges of his hair beneath his white Stetson. Holichek turned to Rusty, who now stood at his side.

"You'd better let him see you, kid. It's your last chance."

Rusty drew in a long breath, moved slowly across the sidewalk, and into the street. Bandine saw him, and his great frame straightened in the saddle. But he did not stop his horse till it was opposite Rusty. In the hot, cottony silence of noon father and son stared at each other without speaking.

Finally Rusty said: "You're going to run?"

"I wouldn't be here if I wasn't. You better go on home."

It took a long time for Rusty's answer to come. "I told you how that was yesterday, Dad. And it's not only me. Every fence cutter in the brush is waiting. If you go through with this, there won't be a fence left standing in the whole county."

"I've already been told that," Bandine said in a thick voice. "They won't stop me with those kinds of threats. I passed Friar and his whole posse on the road. If the fence cutters cut one wire, they'll be in the middle of a war."

"If they are, I'll be with them."

Holichek saw the color leave Bandine's cheeks, till they had a putty hue in the bright light. "Don't talk like a fool," he said. "Friar and Innes are out for blood. Whoever doesn't get killed in the fight will find himself up at Huntsville with Santero. You're not going to get mixed up in it, Rusty. Now stop talking like a fool kid and go on home."

"When will you stop thinking of me as a kid?" The boy's voice broke. "How can I show you I mean what I say? I won't see you sacrifice Santero for the Double Bit, Dad. If I have to join the fence cutters to stop you, I will."

Holichek saw Bandine's eyes grow blank with rage. He knew that this was the moment. Bandine must finally realize that he would lose his son if he went on. He wouldn't sacrifice the boy to that.

Holichek took his cigar from his mouth, waiting for Bandine to speak. But Bandine only stared at Rusty, that blankness in his eyes, that dead-white look to his face. Then, with a sound of rage, he raked his huge Mexican spurs across his horse's flanks, jolting it into a gallop that took him in a swirling cloud of dust to the hotel where Guthrie was staying. Without looking back, he pulled up his horse and swung off, dropping the reins across the rack, and disappeared through the door.

Holichek's whole expectancy had been reversed so suddenly that it did not register for a moment. His mind blank with shock, he watched Rusty standing in the street for what seemed an eternity, staring after his father. Then the boy came back to his horse. As if from a great distance, Holichek saw the utter misery in his face. One by one, Garrison and Tevis and Revere

184

passed Holichek, each glancing at his blank face. Farther down the street, other men were mounting. Rusty climbed into his saddle, sent one last despairing glance at the hotel, then wheeled his horse and kicked it into a dead run out of town.

Only then did Holichek's defeat begin to reach him. He dropped his cigar, staring emptily at it on the splintered planking of the sidewalk. He began to feel sick to his stomach.

The Trowbridge case had been canceled that morning, and it left nothing on Nadell's docket till afternoon. He had slept late and eaten breakfast about 11:00. He knew the whole town was waiting to see if Bandine would come in, and was at the inn door when the man appeared. He had seen the meeting between father and son in the street, had seen Rusty leave with Garrison and Tevis and the others. As the dust of their running horses settled back into the street, he started across toward O'Hara's *cantina*. He knew that Holichek was inside and wanted to talk with the man, feeling that there was something about this he did not yet fully understand.

He was halfway across when he saw Bandine emerge from the hotel and start up toward O'Hara's. He still limped noticeably. Knowing how the man felt, Nadell had the impulse to turn back to the inn. But Bandine had already seen him. The expression on the man's face was not what Nadell had seen in their other chance meetings since Kit's death. There was no anger, no hurt, no blame in his eyes. Only a lost, searching look that made Nadell halt, then go on to wait for the man at the curb. As Bandine approached, Nadell asked quietly: "Are you going to be my opposition now?"

Bandine halted by one of the peeled cottonwood supports, the top of his Stetson almost touching the overhang. He frowned blankly at Nadell for a moment, a slack look to his face. Then he said thickly: "I didn't sign with Guthrie."

It was a complete surprise to Nadell. He knew Bandine and the other big operators fully expected ruin if the fence bill was not passed this year. "What on earth happened?" he asked.

Bandine looked down at the walk, still frowning intensely, as if seeking to understand what had occurred within him. "Adah told me once, a long time ago, that I'd lose my kids if I didn't stop this scramble to get big. She was right, Major. I guess I didn't realize that till just now. But it was more than my scramble losing them. It was the things inside me. I get awful mad sometimes, don't I?"

Nadell nodded sober agreement. "You do."

"And pride. I got so much pride it chokes me. Those are the things that always spoiled it, with Rusty. It's what happened just now. I got so mad at him I couldn't talk. My own son, threatening to turn on me that way. It fair burned me up. I didn't realize how wrong I was till I started up those stairs to Guthrie's room. Then everything started coming back. All the times I'd lost Rusty and Kit, all the little things and big things. Like that time in town when I fought with Holichek and the Davis police dragged me in. I should have known Holichek was just goading me. If I hadn't let him do it, I could've bought the ponies for the kids like I promised. And if I hadn't gotten mad at Kit and driven her away, she might be alive right now."

"You mustn't blame yourself for that."

Bandine did not seem to hear him. He was staring beyond Nadell now. "Waggoner said he could get Santero off. But Rusty said that Waggoner might be wrong. And Rusty was right. That's what came to me, going up those stairs. Santero's an old man, a broken man. If he has to stay at Huntsville it'll kill him, just like Rusty said. I can't take that chance. I hold Santero's life in my hands, just like I held Kit's, and I can't sacrifice him for all the money or all the beef in the world. If I hadn't been so damn' mad and so damn' proud and so crazy to get big, I would have

186

seen that long before this." He looked at Nadell, as if seeking confirmation, then said: "I've got to go home and tell Rusty that, Major."

"I don't think he rode home, Emery. He went out with Garrison and Tevis and those others."

Bandine's eyes went blank. Then he let out in a great gust. "You're crazy. He wouldn't go with them. That was just wild kid talk. He wouldn't really turn on me that way. . . ."

"You've faced all the rest, why can't you face this? Rusty is grown up. If he's going to join the fence cutters, he must think this is the only way to stop you."

Bandine frowned at Nadell, until it reached him fully, and then said all in a burst: "Which way did they go, where are they gathering?"

"I don't know, Emery. . . ."

A wild look crossed Bandine's face. He wheeled to stare at the saloon door. Then, with an inarticulate sound of rage, he lunged through the batwings. Nadell followed him and saw him heading through the dim room toward Holichek, who sat at the farthest table in the room. Holichek's head raised listlessly. Nadell thought he had never seen such defeat in any man's face. Holichek's mouth was slack with it; his eyes were glazed and blank. He seemed to dredge up surprise with great effort. Bandine reached the table and put his palms flat on the top, leaning all his weight onto them.

"Holichek," he said, "where are those fence cutters gathering?"

Some of the wildness in Bandine's face reached Holichek, and his whole broad frame pressed itself against the chair back. "I don't know," he said.

"You do know. Garrison's your man and he's been a maver-icker and a fence cutter for years. You've been hand in glove with every attempt to cut the big operators down."

Holichek's chair scraped shrilly against the floor as he slid it back. "Bandine, you're crazy. . . ."

Bandine took his palms off the table and began to circle it. "These fence cutters are going to start a war out there, Holichek. If Rusty don't get killed in it, he'll be sent to Huntsville with all the rest. I couldn't stop that any more than I could stop Santero being sent there. You've been building Rusty up to this for a long time. Did you think I was blind? You've been cultivating him and poisoning his mind and working him toward this day for years. You knew that, when it came to a choice between my son and everything I'd built, I couldn't sacrifice Rusty."

Bandine stopped by Holichek's chair. The other man had backed against the wall. All the blood was drained from his swarthy cheeks, leaving them sallow, making his eyes seem even blacker. But there was no fear in them, only a watchful, predatory waiting. Nadell knew why the man could not tell. If he revealed the fence cutters' gathering place now, they would look upon it as a betrayal and he would lose their friendship for good. Bandine's voice lowered, till it was barely audible to Nadell.

"Are you going to tell me, Holichek?"

"I don't know, Bandine."

Without a sound Bandine threw himself at the man. Holichek flipped his coattail up and tried to draw his gun. But Bandine's rush carried him into the man before Holichek could get the weapon free. It smashed Holichek against the wall so hard the whole building shuddered. Nadell called to them and started forward in an impulse to stop it. But O'Hara had come around the bar and he grabbed Nadell's arm.

"Don't get in there, Major. You'll only get hurt. This has been coming for fifteen years, and Hood's own brigade couldn't stop it."

Holding Holichek against the wall, Bandine twisted his gun

arm till Holichek had to drop the weapon with a hoarse sound of pain. Then Bandine tried to release one of his hands to hit Holichek. It gave the other man enough freedom to lunge into Bandine before he could strike. It knocked Bandine backward, still holding onto Holichek's arm with one hand, pulling Holichek with him as they staggered away from the wall and into a table.

It skidded from beneath Bandine and he fell, pulling Holichek down, too. It broke his hold, however, and Holichek fell away from him, sprawling flat. Holichek rolled over and tried to scramble erect and get away from Bandine at the same time. Bandine lunged after him from one knee, catching his coat.

The coat ripped down the back and Holichek's impetus pulled him out of half of it, leaving the empty piece of garment in Bandine's hand. The sudden release sent Holichek staggering in his original direction, until he came against a table. Dropping the coat, Bandine plunged after him. Holichek wheeled around, setting himself, meeting Bandine with a blow to the belly. Bandine took it with a sick grunt and went on into Holichek, smashing him fully across the face. It bent Holichek violently back over the table. Bandine grabbed him and held him there, hitting him across the face again, shouting at him: "Where is Rusty, Holichek?"

Holichek rolled to the side and kicked Bandine in the bad leg. Nadell saw pain contort Bandine's face, as his leg went from beneath him, and he fell heavily. Breathing gustily, blood dripping from his black beard, Holichek swung around to grab a nearby chair. Bandine was trying to get up and had gained his hands and knees when Holichek wheeled back and smashed the chair down on his head. It brought an outraged shout from Nadell.

The chair shattered across Bandine's back and head, leaving only a stout rear leg in Holichek's hand. As he shifted to bring this lethal club down on Bandine's head again, Bandine twisted around dazedly, gaining one knee and throwing an arm up to block the blow.

Nadell gasped at the sickening sound of wood striking flesh and bone. It knocked Bandine back down but allowed him a chance to grab the club before Holichek could recover, giving it a desperate jerk. Holichek did not let go soon enough and it pulled him bodily into Bandine, flipping him over the man to sprawl heavily on the floor beyond.

Still stunned from the blow with the chair, Bandine crawled blindly to the bar. He got his hands on the mahogany top and pulled himself to his feet. Then he turned around, hooking his elbows over the edge of the bar, and hung there, sucking in great breaths, waiting for Holichek to rise.

Holichek had already rolled over, shaking his head. He got to his hands and knees, sending one blank look around for his club. Then his eyes reached Bandine. He crouched there a moment, staring balefully at the man, the breath passing gustily in and out of his broad chest. Then he got to one knee and started backing up so that he would be out of Bandine's reach when he rose. Bandine realized his intent and threw himself away from the bar at the man. Holichek tried to jump to his feet, but Bandine reached him before he was fully erect.

His first blow caught Holichek solidly, swinging him around to fall heavily against the bar. Bandine lunged after the man and struck again. Nadell saw Holichek's face go white with shock. It straightened him back against the bar, and Bandine moved in close, hitting him again and again. It was punishment no man could stand long. Holichek made a feeble effort to block the blows, but Bandine swept his arms aside and sank his fist deeply into the man's belly.

With a retching sound, Holichek tried to wheel away, but Bandine caught his torn and bloody shirt, pulling him back and pinning him to the bar with another blow. Holichek's face contorted and his whole body went slack and he fell helplessly against Bandine. The red-headed man held him up, gasping: "Where is he, Holichek?"

Holichek's groaning sound was muffled against Bandine's shirt, and he tried to push free without answering. Bandine caught him by the shirt with both hands and swung him violently around. The back of Holichek's knees struck a chair and he fell into it, slack as a rag doll. The only thing that kept him from sliding away was Bandine's grip on his shirt. Bandine was almost as spent, and barely kept from falling across the man. He hit him again, across the face. "Where, Holichek?"

The words made a husky, sobbing sound in the room. Holichek lunged feebly up against Bandine, pawing at his hands. Bandine smashed him across the face once more, one side, and then the other. Holichek's head jerked violently to the left and to the right, and then lolled slackly over the chair back. His face was loose with shock, his mouth gaping open, a thin flow of blood leaking from his cut mouth into his soggy spade beard.

"Where?" Bandine gasped.

Holichek started to slide limply out of the chair. Bandine jerked him up. Holichek's glazed eyes finally opened, staring at the savagery of Bandine's face, at the fist held to strike again. Holichek's lips moved, but for a moment no sound came out. Finally Nadell heard it. "Mexican Thickets."

Bandine stared blankly at him, the hoarse sound of their breathing the only noise in the room for a moment. Then Bandine wheeled around, almost pitched on his face, and staggered toward the door. He had to stop near the front end of the bar, hanging there a moment, to get the strength to go on. Then he stumbled out through the batwings and disappeared.

O'Hara went behind the bar for some gin and took it to Holichek. The man spewed up some of it and was sick. Nadell stood by the bar, feeling a thin nausea in reaction to the primitive violence of the fight. O'Hara gave Holichek another drink and he got it all down and a little color returned to his cheeks.

"So you were doing that," Nadell said then. "You were using a man's own son against him."

Holichek coughed weakly, wiped blood from his mouth. "Don't listen to that crazy Bandine. The important thing is that he didn't sign with Guthrie. You're in, Major. We'll be calling you senator now."

"If you'd use a man's own son against him, to gain your ends up here, what would you use down in Austin, to gain your ends?"

Holichek raised his head, staring blankly at Nadell. "What?"

"My daughter tried to tell me how you and Bob really operated a long time ago. I guess I had to see it for myself. I feel as though I've been a child, Holichek, and I've just grown up. You'll have to find yourself another man."

Holichek tried to rise, failed miserably. "Don't talk like that. With Bandine out of it, we'll have everything our way. But it won't do any good without you. The fence cutters were our big weapon. When they find out I told where they were gathering, we'll lose them for good. All we have left is you."

"Then you haven't got anything left," Nadell said, "because I'm through with you."

XXI

There was something sly and secretive about the crackle of brush as it parted before the passage of the seven riders. Afternoon sunlight spun a honeyed haze through the mats of chaparral, its heat drawing a rancid scent of rotting mesquite beans from the deep layer of decay on the ground. Mexican Thickets lay only a half mile ahead, and Rusty could see the knowledge reflect a growing tension in the faces of his six companions. They had been riding a game trace that had forced them to travel single file for an hour, but now they broke into a pear flat, and Garrison and Revere dropped back to flank Rusty, while Graves and Tevis and the two Mexicans bunched up from the rear. Rusty had ridden all the way in miserable silence, trying to down all the conflict his decision had brought. Finally he could bear it no longer, and asked Revere: "Do you really think this will do it, Revere? So many fences have been pulled down, it hasn't stopped them. . . ."

"But never like this, *amigo*," the half-breed said, putting a reassuring hand on Rusty's shoulder. "Never the whole countryside rising up as one man and swearing not to stop till every fence in the land is pulled down. We must save Santero somehow. We must save ourselves. This is the only weapon we have left."

Rusty shook his head, recalling all the other times he had heard those arguments. Out in the thickets with some gathering of sun-blackened brushpoppers whose cattle had died of thirst because fences cut off their water. In the smoky torchlight of O'Hara's *cantina,* with Holichek's husky voice in his ear, surrounded by the dark and sweating faces of men whose comradeship was based on the cause. It had all seemed gallant and conspiratorial then, a cause worth fighting for. To Rusty, his father and the big operators had been completely wrong, completely unjustified. But now, as Revere went on talking, he found the doubts stirring.

"I, too, did not think your father would go ahead and see Guthrie when he knew it meant you would join us, Rusty. But I guess we did not realize how truly blind with power Emery had become. . . ."

He broke off at the distant crackle of thickets, and all the men began checking their horses, turning in their saddles. Rusty wore no revolver, but had a Winchester booted under his left stirrup leather. He realized that his hand was touching its butt plate.

"None of Friar's men would be fool enough to make that much noise," Tevis said.

"Might be my brother," Billy Graves muttered. "He stayed in town to see what happened when Bandine came down."

The crash of brush grew louder and the horses began tossing their heads and fiddling. The smell of their sweat began to fill the clearing, sour and rank, and there was a muted creak of rigging as the men shifted uneasily in their saddles.

"We better pull into the brush," Garrison said.

Graves shook his head. "It must be Lee. This is the only way we'd take to Mexican Thickets and he's the only one coming from that direction that would know it."

Garrison jerked his horse around and started for the protection of brush anyway, but they had quarreled too long. With a last cannonade of crashing brush, the rider burst into the pear flat. Rusty felt himself lift in the saddle as he recognized his father on a roan he had run almost to death. Bandine leaned back against his reins and wheeled his animal toward them, pulling it to a halt. He almost had to shout to be heard over the roar of its labored breathing.

"Rusty, get out of here! Holichek spilled the beans! The whole town must know where the fence cutters are gathering by now! It'll get out to Friar and he's liable to come down on you any time!"

Rusty settled back into his saddle, bitterness giving a gray, aged look to his face. "You can't get me out now, Dad. You finished it when you signed with Guthrie."

Bandine put the spurs to his horse, jumping it toward them. "I didn't sign with Guthrie, jigger."

It ran through Rusty like a spasm. He leaned forward in the saddle, searching his father's face for the truth. Bandine was almost among them, and Tevis kicked his horse out to flank the man, hand on his gun. Garrison edged his animal in on Bandine's other side, saying to Rusty: "Don't listen to him, kid. We all saw him go in that hotel. He's probably got a hundred men out in the thickets. He's just trying to get you away before it starts."

"We haven't time to argue," Bandine said. "No telling how soon the news will reach the sheriff. He'll be coming this way to Mexican Thickets. I can't let you be caught in it, Rusty. I didn't sign with Guthrie. You've got to believe me."

Rusty had never heard his father plead with anyone before, but the man was doing it now; he might as well have been on his knees. It shook the resolve in the youth. Garrison saw him wavering and cursed thinly.

"It's a trick, I tell you." His dark face turned to Tevis, who had edged his horse to within a couple of feet of Bandine's flank. "Get his gun, Tevis!"

The man reined his horse hard into Bandine's lathered roan, grabbing for Bandine's six-shooter. He got it out but Bandine wheeled to catch his wrist and heave upward on it. The leverage twisted Tevis right off his horse. At the same time Bandine saw Garrison go for his gun and spurred his roan at the man. The spooky animal quartered heavily into Garrison's horse, allowing Bandine to knock the man's arm up as his gun came free. Unable to shoot Bandine, Garrison brought his gun arm back down in a violent motion that whipped the heavy weapon brutally across Bandine's face. With a hoarse cry Bandine pitched backward out of the saddle.

The roan reared up, blocking the fallen man off from Garrison, who tried to rein his dancing horse around the roan's rump for a clear shot at Bandine. As Rusty realized the man's intent, he yanked his Winchester from its boot, snapping the finger lever and shouting: "Garrison, stop it!"

The man whirled spasmodically in his saddle, saw Rusty's gun, and fired. But his pirouetting horse threw his aim off and the bullet went wild. Rusty squeezed his trigger and saw it strike Garrison's shoulder, tearing him around and out of the saddle.

Tevis had rolled over on the ground, dazedly pawing for his six-shooter. Rusty whipped the Winchester toward him, and Tevis froze. The gun covered the other riders, also, aborting whatever they had meant to do. Rusty lifted his left leg over the horn and slid off, facing them. Then he went to his father, holding them with the threat of his gun. Bandine's face was covered with blood and he lay inert as a dead man. Sick and trembling, Rusty spoke to Tevis.

"Throw him over his horse. I'm getting him out of here."

Emery Bandine regained consciousness in the hovel of Santero Morales, with the old man's hand-carved saints staring at him from every corner. There were other faces—Doc Ainsworth, Chico Morales, Rusty, Claire.

"I must've been out a long time," Bandine said feebly.

Claire sat at the head of the bunk, touching his bandaged face tenderly. "The doctor kept you under sedatives through the night. That whack Garrison gave you almost finished the job Holichek started. After Rusty got you away, Billy Graves told the fence cutters you hadn't signed with Guthrie. It stopped them till Dad reached them and convinced them it was true. He's sure Santero will get off if fence cutting isn't a felony."

Chico stood above Bandine, half frowning, half smiling. "Maybe that stops the big war, but the cutting will go on, Emery. You knew that. You knew what you were sacrificing when you turned Guthrie down. It don't matter whether it's mavericking or another bad winter, the Double Bit is finished."

"And I did it for Santero, if that's what you mean," Bandine said. "Santero and Rusty. I guess I couldn't lose either of them, when I came right down to it. Nothing was worth that." He looked up at Rusty. "So we're out in brush again, jigger. Only the shirts on our backs."

"You know it doesn't matter," Rusty said. "Not as long as we're together again."

Bandine chuckled gruffly to hide the emotion in him. "Now I guess you'll have to be a lawyer," he said.

He saw the last bit of doubt flee the boy's face, saw one of Rusty's rare grins light his eyes. It made him remember, somehow, what Chico had said, long ago. *He is a boy, and you are a man. Until he grows up, that gap will always stand between you.* Well, Rusty was grown up now. He was a man. The rest of it was up to Bandine. He couldn't mend a lifetime of mistakes in a minute. But he had made a good start today. He felt infinitely nearer to the boy than he had been this morning. And he could see the kinship reflected in the boy's face. It would still be a long road, but he was on the right track at last.

Finally Doc Ainsworth said Bandine needed peace and quiet and asked them to clear out. When the doctor saw Claire hesitating at the door, he pulled on his goatee and grinned and gave her five minutes. After he was gone, Claire remained at the door, studying Bandine darkly.

"Rusty's made me see a lot today," Bandine said. "If I'd gone on being so blind and stubborn, I would have lost him the same as I lost Kit. It made me realize I was to blame for her death as much as Webb. I can't hold it against any of you any more."

She came to him, breathing his name, sitting beside him and taking him into her arms. "You must never leave me again, Emery. You'll start today. You'll come to our home until you're well."

He smiled broadly. "Yes, ma'am."

She pouted at him. "And since we're almost man and wife,

must you go on being so infernally polite to me?" He pulled her down to kiss her. "No, ma'am," he said.

ABOUT THE AUTHOR

Les Savage, Jr. was born in Alhambra, California and grew up in Los Angeles. His first published story was "Bullets and Bullwhips" accepted by the prestigious magazine, Street & Smith's *Western Story.* Almost ninety more magazine stories followed, all set on the American frontier, many of them published in Fiction House magazines such as *Frontier Stories* and *Lariat Story Magazine* where Savage became a superstar with his name on many covers. His first novel, *Treasure of the Brasada,* appeared from Simon & Schuster in 1947. Due to his preference for historical accuracy, Savage often ran into problems with book editors in the 1950s who were concerned about marriages between his protagonists and women of different races—a commonplace on the real frontier but not in much Western fiction in that decade. Savage died young, at thirty-five, from complications arising out of hereditary diabetes and elevated cholesterol. However, as a result of the censorship imposed on many of his works, only now are they being fully restored by returning to the author's original manuscripts. Among Savage's finest Western stories are *Fire Dance at Spider Rock* (Five Star Westerns, 1995), *Medicine Wheel* (Five Star Westerns, 1996), *Coffin Gap* (Five Star Westerns, 1997), *Phantoms in the Night* (Five Star Westerns, 1998), *The Bloody Quarter* (Five Star Westerns, 1999), *In The Land of Little Sticks* (Five Star Westerns, 2000), *The Cavan Breed* (Five Star Westerns, 2001), *Danger Rides the River* (Five Star Westerns, 2002), and *Black Rock Cañon*

(Five Star Westerns, 2006). Much as Stephen Crane before him, while he wrote, the shadow of his imminent death grew longer and longer across his young life, and he knew that, if he was going to do it at all, he would have to do it quickly. He did it well, and, now that his novels and stories are being restored to what he had intended them to be, his achievement irradiated by his powerful and profoundly sensitive imagination will be with us always, as he had wanted it to be, as he had so rushed against time and mortality that it might be. *Satan's Keyhole* will be his next Five Star Western.